W9-APR-249
WITHDRAWN

Also by Mark Binder

Autobiographical Lies

Tall Tales, Whoppers and Lies

Dead at Knotty Oak

Crumbs Don't Count
(The Rationalization Diet)

Adventures with Slugs

Folk Tales

The Bed Time Story Book

Classic Stories for Boys and Girls

Adventures with Giants

The Chelm Series

The Council of Wise Women

The Brothers Schlemiel

A Hanukkah Present

A Chanukah Present (audio)

The World's Best Challah

The Brothers Schlemiel from
Birth to Bar Mitzvah (audio)

It Ate My Sister

Mark Binder

Light Publications

Edited by Beth Hellman
Design consultation by Claudia Summer
Copyediting by Patty Tanalski
Front cover illustration and black and white images
Copyright 2008 Jupiterimages Corporation

"The P.I. Kid" and "The Bully and the Shrimp" were first published in *Cricket Magazine.*
A version of "It Ate My Sister" was recorded on *Dead at Knotty Oak.*
An early audio version of "Abu Hassan's Mighty Wind" was recorded as part of *Classic Stories for Boys and Girls,* but was omitted for prurient reasons. It is available on iTunes.
"Ellen vs. the Snakes" was written and first published and recorded for the Seekonk Public Library Summer Program, 2008.

Thanks to my kids, for listening.

Thanks to Roger Blumberg and Max Apple for the proof copy of "The Jew of Home Depot," which inspired "Runninghead." Thanks to the folks at the Medicine Bow Lodge for inspiring "The Tale of Bad Breath Bill."

ISBN 978-0-9702642-4-4
Printed in the United States of America
10 9 8 7 6 5 4 3 2

Light Publications
PO Box 2462
Providence, RI 02906
U. S. A.
www.lightpublications.com

Have an excellent day!

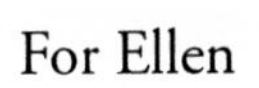

For Ellen

Contents

It Ate My Sister

WHEN I was a kid, I had an older sister. Her name was Ellen, and she was two years older than me. When we were really little, we had played together, but now we didn't get along. We didn't hate each other — we just couldn't stand each other. Everything I did drove her crazy, and everything she did was designed to torture me. Whenever she was on the phone with her friends, she called me a little slug, and she was always on the phone. But the worst thing she did happened every single morning.

Every day I woke up having to go, you know, to the bathroom.

In my house, you went up the stairs and my bedroom was first on the left. My parents' room was up the hall on the right. Ellen's was further up on the left. At the end of the hall was the bathroom.

Every morning, I'd get up and start trudging out down the hall. My mother had put down this red shag carpeting. It looked like a rug made out of bloody worms, but felt good when you stumbled along in bare feet.

Then, just before I got to the bathroom, the door to Ellen's room would pop open. She'd jump inside and slam the door in my face. I swear she was listening. It was like I was her alarm clock.

"Go away, you creep."

"Ellen," I'd groan. "I was here first."

"Obviously you weren't," she'd laugh. "Otherwise you'd be in here, and I'd be out there. But you're not, so there!"

"Ellen, come on. I'll be quick."

There were only two bathrooms in our house. Our bathroom and the one in my parents' bedroom. We were supposed to share our bathroom.

"Go away."

"Please..." I'd beg.

"I'll be right out." She was lying. She'd be in there for like a week.

"Come on," I'd moan.

"Leave me alone."

I'd start banging on the door.

"Mom! Dad!"

By then, my folks were probably doing rock paper scissors to see who would handle the first fight of the day. Dad usually lost. He'd open his door and say, "What's going on around here?"

Just then, the door to the bathroom would pop open, and Ellen would bounce out. "I don't know what his problem is." She'd give him a kiss on the cheek. "Good morning, Daddy!" While she gave him a hug, she'd stick out her tongue at me and mouth the words, "You little slug!" Then she'd bop into her room and slam the door.

She got away with it every time.

This happened every single morning, school day or weekend, rain or shine. I tried tiptoeing. I tried sleeping in. Nothing worked.

At last, I decided to get revenge.

That spring, we were having a science fair in our school. The teachers had assigned us to invent a research project and they were hoping some genius wasn't going to blow up the cafeteria.

That afternoon, my mom came running into the house with her plastic gardening shoes tracking mud everywhere, and yelped that her garden was infested with slugs.

"Perfect!" Ellen said. "Let the little slug take care of his friends."

I smiled. "Okay. I will."

Mom looked both surprised and proud. "You can do whatever you want with the slugs."

That evening, and for the next three nights, I went out after dark with a flashlight, a pair of chopsticks, and a large mason jar, and began harvesting slugs – for scientific experimentation purposes.

Slugs, as you probably know, are basically snails without the shell. They like to come out at night because it's cooler. Their Latin name is *terrestrial gastropod mollusk*, which roughly translates as "one-footed land clam." They like damp places, and have a fondness for eating vegetation of all kinds, especially my Mom's garden. She'd tried everything to get rid of them, but Mom was into organic gardening before it was fashionable, so she wouldn't use pesticides. As a result, that garden had a slew of slugs.

I could have harvested the slimers by picking them up with my fingers, but they hide under leaves, and it was easier to snag them with the chopsticks.

At last, the jar was full. I lifted it up to the moon, stared at the slowly wriggling mass of thirty-nine slugs and let out a wicked laugh.

The next morning, while Ellen was still in the bathroom, I sneaked downstairs and dropped a slug into her orange juice. Then I filled her cereal bowl with slugs and covered it up with a napkin.

By the time she got done getting dressed, I was sitting at the table with the newspaper, pretending to read the comics.

"Good morning, slug."

I shook my newspaper. You don't know the half of it, I thought.

She picked up her juice cup and began to drink.

Glug, glug, glug… "OH MY GOD!"

The cup flew across the room and bounced off the refrigerator. She ran to the sink, rinsed her mouth out, and then gargled.

I lowered the newspaper. "Is everything okay?"

She scowled at me, went back to the table, lifted the napkin up off her cereal bowl, and screamed like she'd stuck her finger into an electrical socket. "OH MY GOD!"

She jumped up on her chair, and was still standing there, screaming and pointing at me when Mom and Dad came running into the kitchen.

"What's going on around here?" Dad asked.

"I'm sorry, my slugs must have escaped!" I said, innocent as a newborn babe. "I'll take them up to my room."

I giggled all the way upstairs. I put the jar on my desk, and then hung a sign on the door. "Science Laboratory DO NOT ENTER."

Now came the fun part.

My science fair project was going to be simple. I was going to take a slug, measure its length, weigh it, and then dump a tablespoon of salt on its back and watch it melt.

The salt sort of works like acid. It dries the slug out, eats through the slug's cell walls, the water and slug guts come oozing out, and it melts down into a puddle of slime. It's disgustingly cool.

I know that it's a horrible thing to kill a living creature, but when you're an ordinary, curious but somewhat sick and twisted lad, slowly turning a slug into a pile of ooze is wicked awesome to watch. Besides, it was my science project. My theory — because you have to have a theory — was that the bigger the slug the longer it would take to melt down. So I did it again and again.

I went through three dozen slugs. I photographed them, made charts and graphs, and wrote down my impressions of their final moments. It was going to be a great science project. All the guys in school were going to be impressed.

Then, one morning, Ellen ignored the warning on my door and walked right into my bedroom.

"Ewww!" she moaned. "That is so gross."

I was making notes that "Subject #38 appears to be trying to escape, but to no avail."

I grinned. "Yeah! "

Ellen scowled. "Did you read the science fair manual?"

"Yes," I lied.

"No you didn't. Did you read rule number seventy-four?"

"Yes, of course!" I lied.

"Rule seventy-four says no cruelty to animals," Ellen said with a smug smile.

I stared at Subject #38. "It's a slug."

"It's still an animal. You're killing it. And it's cruel."

"But Mom said I could do whatever I wanted to the slugs."

"Rule seventy-four says you can't. Your science project is illegal."

She smirked and then flounced out of the room.

I grabbed the rulebook, flipped the pages and read:

> *74. No projects exhibiting any form of cruelty to animals will be accepted.*

Ellen had ruined my science fair project.

I didn't know what to do. Time was running out. The science fair was coming up fast, participation was mandatory, and I needed a new project.

That day at breakfast, I read an article in the paper about the questionable effects of growth hormones in milk on children. Evidently farmers had been putting a genetically modified chemical called recombinant bovine growth hormone, or rBGH, into cows. It made the cows get bigger and fatter quicker, and they produced more milk. The problem was that some of the chemical got into the milk and nobody knew what it did to kids.

Over the course of the day, I began to wonder what it might do to a slug.

That afternoon, when I got home from school, I filled a bottle cap with milk, brought it up to my room, set it in front of a slug, and waited.

If there's one thing more boring than waiting for your sister to get out of the bathroom, it's waiting for a slug to do anything – anything at all. I waited and waited and waited. It started to rain, but the slug wouldn't touch the milk. They need a lot of water to live, but it turns out that slugs don't like milk. Slugs are basically herbivores, which means that they'll eat almost any kind of plant. They do like some really tiny bugs, but evidently milk is not high up on their list of favorite foods.

I thought about injecting it, but I had done such a good job cleaning out the garden that this was my last slug. My mother was pleased that there weren't any pests eating her basil, but I had a problem. The science fair was only days away.

What, I wondered, would my favorite scientist do? Some of the kids in my school idolized Albert Einstein. Some wrote reports on Marie Curie or Jonas Salk. But my favorite scientist has always been Dr. Frankenstein.

At that moment, there was a flash of lightning and a thunderclap. Perfect!

I got a battery, a roll of electrical tape and a couple of wires. I taped the wires to the battery. I put the slug next to the bottle cap full of milk, and then I zapped it.

Whoah! It sucked that milk up like it was drinking through a straw.

I grinned. Was this cruelty? I don't know. The slug didn't make a sound. It didn't even twitch. Maybe I wouldn't win the science fair, but it was still pretty cool.

I went to bed, and the next morning, it seemed to be bigger. I took some measurements and confirmed my hypothesis. It had grown from one inch to two inches. Awesome!

That afternoon, I got a quarter cup of milk from the fridge, wired the slug, and watched it suck that milk in. It blew up to the size of a tennis ball. Wicked! I wondered whether it would retain the weight or excrete it. I was also worried that it might burst. So, rather than feed it more and risk a blowout, I went to bed.

The next morning it had stabilized at four inches. My eyes sparkled. I had some time, so I ran downstairs and filled a two-cup measure. I wrote, "Buy more milk" on the shopping list. Then I ran back upstairs, hooked the slug up to a bigger battery and watched. I could actually see it expand, like a milky water balloon slowly self-inflating.

After school that slug was sixteen inches long, the size of a small cat, and it seemed to be still growing. I gently picked it up. It was like carrying a slab of warm jello. I couldn't weigh it because it oozed off the scale. The science fair was the next day. I imagined myself winning first prize and then accepting the Nobel Prize for biology!

That's when I heard Ellen, laughing on the phone.

Maybe I could win another one for psychological experimentation too…

I carefully carried it down the hall and I knocked on the door to her bedroom with my elbow.

"Hey, Ellen," I giggled, mad scientist-like. "Have you seen my science fair project lately?"

"What do you want?" My sister opened her door.

"You see what happens to little slugs, Ellen? They get bigger."

I lifted it up into her face.

She screamed. Her skin turned dead white and she stumbled back gasping, "Get it away! Get it away!" She started throwing stuffed animals at me, so I got out of there fast, laughing all the way back to my room.

I took lots of pictures of that slug with an instant camera, and waited until nightfall.

It was raining hard that evening, and after everybody had gone to sleep, I sneaked down to the kitchen and swiped the two gallons of milk my mother had just brought from the supermarket. In the attic, I had found a self-refilling water bowl for cats that my folks had bought from an airline catalog. I duct taped the milk jugs onto the cat feeder. I hooked the slug up to the battery, and nothing happened. I tried it again. Still nothing.

I used a voltmeter to check the power level in my battery. It was dead. All my batteries were dead. I was out of power.

Lightning flashed outside my window, and the answer came to me.

I plugged the slug into a wall socket. There was a crack and a spark. The lights in my room flickered and there was a sickly smell. It's a really bad idea to plug anything organic into an electrical outlet.

But it worked! The slug began to drink and to grow. Slowly. Really really slowly. I used a tape measure and a stopwatch. For a while it was swelling an inch every seventeen minutes. Then it stopped for ten minutes. Then it bulged a foot in twenty seconds. Then it paused for an hour. Then it sprouted another nineteen inches in four minutes. Then it stopped again.

My last recorded log entry was a blurry scrawl:

Time: 3:14 am.
Length: 46 inches

I must have fallen asleep, because I had a dream that the slug had grown to the size of the moon, and was slowly wiping out city after city in its search of a giant cow.

The next morning I woke up with my head flat on my desk. I was stiff and tired. Then I remembered. I looked around my room and saw… nothing.

It was gone. For a second, I thought maybe it had exploded, but the walls and ceiling were clean. The door to my bedroom was open. It had escaped.

I jumped up, and almost fell as my feet slid on a puddle of ooze. I slipped and squished to the door.

The hall was empty. The slug hadn't gone down the stairs; they were clean. It had turned left on my Mom's shag carpeting, leaving a trail of slime all the way to the bathroom. That made sense. Slugs need a lot of water.

I hurried as quickly as I could. I felt like I was wading along a stream of warm runny snot. I had to be careful not to slip and fall.

Then, just as I was about to go into the bathroom, the door to Ellen's room popped open, she jumped inside, and slammed the door in my face.

"Ellen!" I yelped.

"Go away, you creep."

"Ellen!" I banged. I rattled the doorknob. Locked.

That's when it hit me. My science project was in the bathroom and my older sister was doing her usual morning torture the kid brother routine.

I grinned. "Ellen, is there something in there with you?"

"What?"

"Ellen, isn't there something big and slimy in there with you?"

"You mean like your face?"

I scowled and shouted. "Have you seen my science fair project lately?"

"No! Now leave me alone!"

No? I didn't understand. Where was it? Where could it be? It was too big for the toilet, or the sink…

"Ellen, don't look in the shower."

"What?"

"Ellen," I said, trying to sound like one of those horror movie trailers, "whatever you do, don't look in the shower."

There was a pause, and a few footsteps. A moment later I heard the plastic clicking sound of the shower curtains being drawn aside and then, "EEIIEEEEEAAAAAAAAAAAAAAAAAAAH!"

I stood to the side so that when she came shooting out of the bathroom she wouldn't knock me into the river of slime. I was having so much fun! I couldn't wait to get my science project to school.

But nothing happened. The door didn't open. What was she doing? I imagined my sister picking up a toothbrush and trying to beat it back. It was an amusing image, but with the slug's skin stretched so thin maybe she might poke a hole in it, and I needed that slug for my exhibit.

"Ellen?" I said. "Open up. I'll come and get it. Ellen?"

I rattled the doorknob. It was locked. "Come on, Ellen. Open up." Still no answer.

I turned and ran down the hall back to my room. As I rounded the corner I slipped and had to bang my hands against the wall to keep from falling. I grabbed a screwdriver, slid back to the bathroom, popped the lock, and opened the door.

Inside was the biggest slug the world has ever seen. Its head was six and a half feet off the ground. Its eye stalks were as thick as my arms, undulating like two giant pythons.

And inside, clearly visible through its bloated milky skin, was my sister.

She had her mouth open in a horrified silent scream. Her arms were flailing, pounding against the slug's viscous insides. Her pink bathrobe seemed to be dissolving. It was digesting her.

There wasn't time to say, "I told you so." I ran out of the bathroom, slipped, fell, and crawled my way to the staircase. I tore downstairs to the front hall where I pulled on a pair of soccer cleats. Then, without tying the laces, I ran into the kitchen and grabbed the salt shaker from the breakfast table.

As I ran back upstairs and down the hall, I unscrewed the shiny metal top.

The slug was looking right at me, its weird eyestalks roving in my direction, and I threw the salt.

It hit the slug in the forehead, right between the eyestalks, and the slug started to hiss and burn and melt.

The slug roared. I never figured out how that slug could make a sound. They don't have vocal cords. It was horrible, like the outraged bellow of a wet lion as it was being squished by a steamroller.

Then it charged.

Fortunately, a slug's charge, even a giant slug's charge, is as slow as, well, a slug. I had plenty of time, though I wasn't sure the same was true for my sister.

I spun around and sprinted back down the hall, down the stairs, through the kitchen and into the garage. I squeezed past my parents' cars and found the blue plastic bucket of rock salt my dad kept for de-icing the driveway in the winter. I grabbed it, ran back upstairs and lugged it down the hall. Grunting and panting I sped back to the bathroom.

The slug was nearly out the door. Ellen's eyes and mouth were closed. Her color didn't look good.

I picked up the bucket in both hands and flung out five gallons of rock salt.

As soon as the salt hit the slug, its thin skin began to sizzle and melt. Its eyestalks twirled in circles. It hissed at me like a punctured tire, as it deflated into a puddle with a sour smell and a final flatulent PHUT.

A slick wave of warm slug slime oozed over my toes.

And standing in the middle of the bathroom, panting and gasping, was my sister, Ellen. She looked horrible. She had slug pus dripping off her forehead, slug snot coming out of her nose, and slug guts coming out of her mouth.

"Are you okay?" I asked, as gently as I could.

"Gaah," was all she could manage. "Gaa-aah."

Just then my parents came out of their bedroom.

"What's going on around here?" my Dad began.

"My new shag carpeting!" Mom said.

Ellen ran into her bedroom and slammed the door.

"Ellen?" Mom and Dad looked frightened.

I tried to explain. I don't think they believed me. Nobody really believed me. Later on, when I showed my photographs at the school science fair, everybody said that I'd just moved a camera closer to a little slug. The science teacher threatened to expel me for falsifying documents. I got an F on my science fair project.

My parents grounded me for a month. I had to clean the bathroom and that shag carpeting was never the same. My best friend David Kovar joked that I'd been charged with assault and battery. I didn't laugh.

My Mom called the milk company and they changed the formula. Don't try it at home. It won't work. You'll just get brown spots on your wall sockets.

But one good thing did happen.

In the mornings, when I got up and went down the hall, if my sister was in the bathroom, all I had to say was, "Ellen, have you seen my science fair project lately?"

She'd be out of there like a shot.

The P.I. Kid

WAY BACK in the days before Nintendo, when I went to camp, they used to call me the P. I. Kid.

It started on an overnight hiking trip. Fifteen miles across pastures and through deep forest to the old deserted Crosby barn, the spookiest ghost-haunted campground in the whole county. It was rumored that a hundred years ago, on that very spot, a farmer had been burned to death by his own daughter.

Twelve campers and two counselors got up at the crack of dawn, ate a disgusting breakfast of creamed chipped beef on toast, and cheerfully marched off down the Red Rock trail singing, "A hundred bottles of beer on the wall!"

By three in the afternoon, we were dragging our feet. Our voices were gone and we were tired, sore and cranky.

"Come on, you slugs!" shouted Alex Leanthouse, a huge counselor nicknamed "The House" because of the extreme danger if he sat on you. "Move it or die!"

Our other counselor, Matty, had no last name as far as we knew. He was quiet, like an Indian tracker, as he guided us through the thick underbrush. Finally, we reached Slippery Rock Ford, the shallowest place to cross the Breakneck River.

"All right, slime molds," The House bellowed. "Take off your shoes and prepare to cross!"

Like nervous soldiers at the Russian Front, we pulled off our hiking boots and waded into the icy stream, gingerly stepping from rock to jagged rock. The water was only about three inches deep, so it wasn't much of a problem.

We had just about navigated the ford, when Matty, who was in the lead, broke his silence, and said barely loud enough for everybody to hear, "Poison ivy."

"WHAT?" The House shouted.

Matty pointed. A shimmering field of three-leafed underbrush covered the shore as far as the eye could see.

"OH, BUG BREATH!" The House yelled, and everyone shook in mortal terror.

Everyone, except me.

You see, I knew that I was immune to the effects of poison ivy. I'd been going to camp for years, and though everybody else had succumbed at one time or another, I had never even once gotten an itch from the plant.

"We're a-gonna haid north," Matty said. "River's not too deep there. Trail's just on th' other side of th' patch, but Ah'm not takin' any chances."

"All right, maggots, about face!" The House bellowed. "Next ford's four miles upstream. Get moving!"

Well, everybody in the party moaned, turned around and headed back to shore.

Except me. I just went straight on ahead toward the other side.

"Where're you goin'?" Matty asked.

"I'll meet you guys," I said. "I'll wait right on the trail."

"WHAT?" hollered The House.

"I'm immune to the effects of poison ivy!"

"Ah wouldn't wanna be in yer skin," Matty said, shaking his long, thin head.

But I'd already made it to the bank. Everyone else had already turned around and was heading back across the river.

There were rumors that the poison ivy in those woods was so deadly that if you burned it in a campfire, and inhaled the smoke, you could die from the itching inside your lungs. I didn't know what all the fuss was about. To me, poison ivy was just a pretty three-leafed plant. In the early summer it was bright green, but by the end of summer, which this was, it was red and green and quite pretty.

I had some time on my hands and wanted to rest while the rest of the group humped through their eight-mile hike. I looked for a place to lie down. The trail was too rocky, and the tree roots in the woods were too bumpy.

The poison ivy was thick, and the patch would make a nice mattress. I wiped my toes off, and dried my feet on the leaves. Then I shucked off my shirt, lay down in that soft bed of leaves, rolled around until I got comfortable, and took a nap.

I don't know how long I dozed, but I popped awake at the distant shout of, "MOVE IT!" By the time everyone else arrived, I was up and waiting, well rested and chipper.

They, on the other hand, were a scraggly bunch of campers and counselors. The water had gone up to their shoulders, and everything they owned was soaked. There had been a briar patch, too, on the other side of that ford so everybody was pretty well scratched up. After hiking almost three extra hours, they just glared at me as I, whistling, joined in the line.

We got to the campsite. We pitched our tents, ate burgers and dogs, toasted marshmallows, and after dinner, snuck into the barn.

There, Matty and The House told us horrifying ghost stories about men with hooks for hands, and whole families dying together in deliberately set bonfires. By the time we crawled into our sleeping bags, our teeth chattered from the cold night, and the thoughts of all the insane killers lurking outside in the woods. We tossed and turned for a long time before falling asleep.

It wasn't until the early part of the morning that the screaming started.

The sky was still as dark as the blackened bottom of an old coffee pot. At first, the moans started softly. Maybe it was just a cat off in the distance. Maybe a coyote or a bear cub. Or maybe a full-grown grizzly.

I heard the noises faintly in my sleep. They started as horrible little squeals, as if someone had cornered a mouse and was torturing it.

I tried to ignore them, but when the groans became louder, I had to wake up.

Something was screaming loud and close.

My heart was leaping in my chest like a Mexican jumping bean. I felt like I was about to explode!

Then my tent mate, David, turned on his flashlight.

I realized that the screaming wasn't coming from outside the tent. It was coming from inside.

It was coming from me! I was the one screaming.

"AHHHHHH!" I screamed even louder. I jumped up in my sleeping bag and started hopping around the tent, my head banging into the low fabric roof.

By now, white as a ghost, David was screaming too.

We tore out of our sleeping bags and scampered out of that tent like two rats from a sinking boat.

All across the camp site, we heard the other kids screaming as well, until everybody was screaming all at the same time.

At just that moment, a huge flashlight beam hit me dead in the face.

"What's going on?" shouted The House.

"I'm on fire!" I yelled. "I'm on fire!"

"Fire!" David screamed. "Fire!"

"Git some water," Matty said.

David grabbed a bucket and ran off toward the creek.

"Roll on the ground!" The House shouted at me.

So, I started rolling on the ground in the dirt. A moment or two later, David ran up and dumped a bucket of water on my head.

And that's when everybody realized that there weren't any flames flickering up off my fingers, or smoke rising up from my hair. Not even any steam.

"I'm still on fire!" I shouted, still rolling around in the now muddy dirt.

Matty told The House to aim his flashlight closer.

That's when they all started laughing.

I didn't know what was so funny, but I soon found out.

"It's poison ivy," Matty said. "He's got 'bout the worst case Ah've ever seen."

Well, I took a deep breath and stopped making a total fool out of myself. My body still felt like it was enveloped in a wall of flame, but since I knew the truth, I wasn't half as afraid.

I stood up and started brushing the dirt and mud off myself, but Matty said, "Hold it. Don't touch. You'll just spread it worse."

That's when I looked down. That's when I saw.

I was covered, head to foot, from fingertip to fingertip, and everywhere in between with the most disgusting and rankling collection of festering poison ivy sores that the world had ever seen.

Worse? It couldn't possibly be worse. I had it on my arms. I had it on my head, on my hands, on my elbows, on my knees, behind my knees, on my stomach, on my back, on my face....

And worst of all were my feet. I had practically danced a jig on that patch of poison ivy, and my feet, the soles, the toes, the tops and the ankles were all one big swollen red blister.

I didn't dare move. I couldn't budge.

"Don't touch him," The House warned. "He's still contagious."

"Git out yer calamine lotion," Matty said, "and roll it to him."

So, one by one, all my friends dug into their backpacks and rolled me their bottles of pink calamine lotion.

I painted six layers all over my body. I dumped it everwhere. The itching had just about died down when

I found out something else — calamine lotion dries hard. I couldn't move. Even if I wanted to, I couldn't budge an inch.

"Are you all right?" Matty asked.

"Matty," I whispered. "I can't move."

"All right. Stay there. We're goin' to bed."

And they left me there, standing next to the burned out campfire. I stayed awake for the rest of the night, terrified of nocturnal critters nibbling around my toes.

The next morning, they fed me breakfast and packed up the tents.

"We gotta go," Matty said.

"Matty," I whispered, "I can't walk."

"That's all right. We'll come back and get you."

And they left me there, in the middle of the woods.

They had to call in a Boy Scout helicopter to fly me back to camp. They lowered a sky hook, looped a rope under my arms, and floated me out of there.

I was flying above the trees. I was looking down at the river. I was still in my underwear.

They lowered me onto the assembly field, right near the flagpole. Somebody got out a hose and washed me off. Threw me a towel.

I had a lot of nicknames after that. Some kids called me "The Flying Pink Mummy" or "Dripping-With-Pus" and a few weeks later they took to calling me "The Human Scab."

But the one that stuck, the one that haunted me for the rest of my life at that camp, was "The P. I. Kid."

That was something I never lived down.

Even now, I think I feel an itch coming on…

My Grandfather's Turkey

MY FATHER was a doctor, and sometimes his patients would give him gifts. Usually they were lame presents like monogrammed golf balls or sculptures made out of old-fashioned iron nails bent into the shape of skiers. Sometimes he got something cool, like a stuffed cougar, but Mom made him donate that to a shelter for disturbed kids.

One year for Thanksgiving, Dad brought home a seventeen-pound turkey. It was plucked, but the head was still attached and Mom screamed when she saw it. She had to pull all the racks out of the oven just to fit it inside. It took forever to cook, and dinner was really really late.

The funniest thing was that we didn't have a lot of company that year. Sitting around the table were me, my Mom, my Dad, my sister Ellen, my Grandma Bea, and my Grandpa Harry.

We were starving. The mashed potatoes were cold, the green beans were cold, and the cranberry sauce was warm. When Mom finally staggered into the dining room carrying the turkey on a platter, Ellen and I cheered and grabbed our forks and knives like savages.

Dad raised his hands. He had that look that said, I'm going to talk for a long time and you don't have much choice about it.

Ellen and I put down our silverware.

He smiled at us and said, "I just want to say that I'm thankful for everything we have, but especially for my wife for cooking the biggest and the best Thanksgiving turkey ever."

My mother looked like she was going to cry, but I don't think it was gratitude so much as exhaustion. She collapsed into her chair and reached for a glass of wine.

Ellen and I said, "Yaay, Mom!" at the same time, and then grabbed our cutlery. Dad picked up the carving knife and fork. My Grandma Bea was nodding and smiling. She already had her bib daintily tucked into her blouse.

My Grandpa Harry was shaking his head.

My father looked at his father.

Grandpa Harry shook his head. "No."

"What?" Dad said.

My grandpa shrugged. "It's not the biggest and best turkey ever."

"Dad what do you know about turkey?" My father pointed the giant meat fork at his father. "Every year for Thanksgiving we didn't have turkey, we had fish."

My Grandpa Harry was an old man. He didn't talk much. He had a belly that was big, the size of a basketball. It was hard as a rock. He always said that it was full of air, but he'd never explain why it wasn't soft and jiggly like most men's guts. He was retired, and his favorite pastime was to sit at the kitchen table, play solitaire, and watch the birds at the feeder outside the kitchen window. He'd sit there for hours not saying a word.

"That's because of the fish," he began…

"When I was a boy, I worked as a printer's apprentice up in Boston. It was hard work, but my family needed the money. I did all the jobs that the men in the shop didn't want to do. I swept the floors, I cleaned the presses, I put away all the pieces of type in the cases. In the winter, the shop was freezing, and in the summer it was hot. There was no air conditioning back then. I already knew how to read and write and add, so I didn't go to school. We worked six days a week, and I was there from dawn until dark.

"But every summer I got to spend two weeks at my Uncle Ike and Aunt Sadie's farm in Exeter, Rhode Island. That was hard work too, but it was a different kind. I was outside in the fields, or inside in the barn or the chicken coop. And when the chores were done, I used to take my fishing pole down to the pond and do nothing at all. I'd sit on the end of the dock with my bare feet in the water and the line dangling and watch the birds.

"I never caught anything. In that pond, it was nearly impossible to catch anything because there was only one fish in the water. He was a pond trout named Harvey. Over the years, Harvey had grown big and strong and fat and smart. He'd eaten all the other fish in the pond. There weren't even any frogs near that pond because Harvey had eaten all of them. He only ate worms when he wasn't eating small careless seagulls. When he took your worm, you'd feel a quick tug on the line and if you weren't careful, he'd yank the pole right out of your hands. If you did manage to hang onto the pole, the fishing line would snap. And if it didn't snap, then Harvey would somehow unhook the worm and swim off. He was a brilliant giant of a fish.

"It didn't bother me, though. I wasn't brought up to relax and do nothing, and fishing – or rather sitting and fishing – was about as near to heaven as I could imagine.

"One year for Thanksgiving, Uncle Ike invited the whole family down to the farm for dinner. He called it a reunion, but really it was a show-off.

"Uncle Ike had bought a brand-new Glenwood gas stove. It was covered with this algae green enamel and fueled with propane. He got all the men to lug the old cast iron stove out to the back yard.

"Then he went into the shed and brought out a thirty-two pound turkey. The stove was amazing, but the turkey was even more amazing. You couldn't have cooked a turkey that size in that old stove fueled by wood and coal. But now they were "cooking with gas!" Anything was possible.

"While the turkey was cooking, all the women gathered in the kitchen to chop and chatter. All the men gathered in the parlor to play canasta. All the little kids were fooling around with jacks and push cars.

"Me, I wanted to get outside. In those days New England Thanksgivings were cold. There was snow on the ground and ice on the pond and I wanted to go ice skating.

"If I had one vice as a youngster beside fishing it was ice skating. I loved to skate. I'd managed to save up some money and bought myself a pair of skates, and in the winter, every chance I got, before or after work, I'd sneak out to the lake near the print shop and take a turn.

"Now, I knew even then that it's foolishly dangerous to go ice skating by yourself, so I went from room to room and asked around for someone to come with me down to the pond. No one wanted to leave the house. The women were gossiping, the men were gambling, and the little kids said it was too cold outside.

"It made me so mad. A beautiful day, perfect for skating. Plenty of time, with the sun still high and dinner far off on the horizon.

"I stalked out of the kitchen back door, and started kicking my feet through the snow. Giant clods of snow went flying. Then I spotted something odd flipping end over end. It was a red cylindrical tube with a piece of string on one end.

"It looked like a firecracker.

"Later on, I found out that in October, Uncle Ike had been blowing up tree stumps with blasting caps. But even if I'd known, I doubt I would have done anything differently, because I already had an idea for a wicked prank.

"Let me be clear. I am not advocating this. When I was a boy, I did foolish things, and I am lucky to have survived and to still have all my fingers and eyes.

"I dug through the snow and found the firecracker. Then I sneaked in the back door to the kitchen. I drifted over to the stove and pretended to warm my hands.

"When no one was looking, I yanked open the oven door, and shoved the firecracker deep into the turkey, right into the stuffing. I yanked my nearly-burning hand out, shut the oven, and looked around.

"No one had noticed. Then I rushed to the sink and rinsed the hot stuffing from my hands with cool water.

"For a while I lingered in the kitchen, but my mother and Aunt Sadie shooed me outside. For another while I hung around the back door to the kitchen, waiting.

"It occurred to me that although the oven was hot, if the turkey didn't burn then the fuse might not catch on fire and my firecracker might not explode. It also occurred to me that if it did explode, I'd look pretty suspicious standing around the back door waiting.

"So I did my second foolishly stupid thing of the day.

"I went to the car, grabbed my ice skates, and walked down the hill to the pond and onto the dock.

"At the end of the dock there was a ladder leading down into the water for swimming in the summer. The pond was nearly frozen, but there was a small circle of open water right next to the ladder. Probably Uncle Ike had cut it for the ice box. On the other side of the open water, maybe about three feet from the dock, the pond was frozen and the ice looked solid.

"I sat down, took off my boots and put on my skates.

"I teetered to the end of the dock, climbed down one rung, and then jumped across the open water onto the ice.

"It didn't break. The ice creaked, but it held. I was dumb, but I was lucky. At least for a while.

"I started to skate.

"It was a magnificent day. The sky was clear and blue. It was cold but not windy. The farm was covered in white. The fields were smooth, and the stone walls looked as old as the world.

"You can't imagine how fabulous it felt for a city boy used to sneaking out in the dark for a few minutes of skating to glide and twirl and backpedal in the middle of the country with nothing but the sun and breeze for company.

"I was on the far end of the pond when the ice cracked and broke.

"I fell into the water and it felt like all of the life was being sucked out of me. I tried to scream, but I couldn't get any air. Besides, I was on the far end of the pond at the bottom of the hill. Everyone else was inside talking and shouting and making a tumult of noise.

"I tried to scramble out, but as soon as it got wet, the ice got slick. That's why you don't go ice skating alone. You can't climb out by yourself, and you don't have a lot of time. Hypothermia, when your body temperature drops below the point that you can survive, takes only a matter of minutes, and I didn't have long.

"That's when I remembered the ladder at the end of the dock.

"The pond wasn't that big. If I could get to the ladder, I could climb out.

I took a whole bunch of deep breaths, filled my belly up with air, pushed myself under the ice, sank to the bottom, and started to run along the bottom of the pond as fast as I could.

"I wasn't moving fast enough. The blades of my ice skates were sticking into the muck at the bottom of the pond. I didn't think I would make it all the way to the ladder, so I turned around and plowed my way back to the hole I'd fallen through.

"I gasped for breath, and before my fingers could completely freeze up, I yanked off my ice skates, tied the laces together, and threw them over my shoulder so I could carry them with me. The weight would help me sink, and besides, those were my ice skates. I'd bought them with my own money.

"I filled my belly with air, pushed myself under the ice, sank to the bottom and ran as if my life depended on it. Which it did.

"I was only about five feet from the ladder. I could see the bottom rung. I was just reaching out… Then I felt a tug.

"I looked over my shoulder and saw a gigantic fish swimming with my ice skate caught in its mouth.

"It was Harvey. He'd seen the skate flapping along behind me. He hadn't seen a real fish in years, so he'd taken the bait.

"I wasn't about to let go. That was my ice skate. I'd paid for it with my own money, so I held on tightly to my other ice skate and gave it a big yank.

"The blade of the ice skate set in Harvey's cheek and he took off.

"I tried to keep going, but Harvey hauled me off my feet.

"I was being dragged around under the pond backwards. We went around and around. My head kept bumping on the bottom of the ice.

"Just before I completely ran out of breath, Harvey swam close enough to the dock for me to grab a hold of the ladder.

"The fingers of my left hand closed around the bottom rung in vice grip. My other hand hung onto my ice skate. Those were my ice skates. I'd paid good money for them, and I was not going to leave them in the pond. I held on to the rung and pulled on my skate. The wet shoelace gave me enough slack to climb up another rung. I gave the skate another pull and climbed up another rung. Pull, climb! Pull, climb!

"The pond wasn't deep, and the ladder was short. My head broke through into fresh air. I climbed onto the dock, and I gasped for breath.

"That's when I realized I'd landed Harvey. The ice skate lace hadn't broken. It was a short battle as I dragged Harvey up the ladder, out of the pond, and onto the dock.

"He flopped and he flapped, but I didn't let go. He stared me in the eyes and I stared at him right back. I couldn't believe it.

"Harvey was seven feet, six and three-quarters inches long. He was the largest fresh water fish ever caught in the State of Rhode Island and Providence Plantations.

"He was still twitching with my ice skate caught in his maw while I dragged him up the hill to the back door.

"I had my hand on the knob when

"—BOOOOOOM!

"A thirty-two pound turkey came flying out the kitchen and through the back door. It slid down the hill, shot off the end of the dock, and skidded onto the ice where it spun around for a moment until it melted a hole and sank into the water with a mushroom cloud hiss of steam.

"The farmhouse was in chaos. Uncle Ike was terrified that the propane gas tanks were going to explode. Aunt Sadie was in tears. She was wailing.

"'What are we going to feed everyone for Thanksgiving dinner?'

"I lifted up my ice skate and held Harvey as high as I could.

"'We'll have fish.'

"Our family reacts well in a crisis. Uncle Ike disconnected the propane. Aunt Sadie fired up the old cast-iron stove, and Harvey made us a meal to be thankful for."

We all sat silent and still for a moment.

"And that," explained my Grandpa Harry, "is why we always had fish for Thanksgiving dinner."

My Dad didn't know what to say. He looked at his father. Then he looked at his mother. "Ma, is that true?"

My Grandma Bea pursed her lips and said in her quiet way, "I don't know if it is true or not. He told me that story when we got married, and made me cook fish every year. I am just so thankful that I can finally have turkey for Thanksgiving dinner!"

The Bully and the Shrimp

BUTCH MATTINGLY was the biggest kid in the fifth grade at Fernwood Elementary. He'd been the biggest kid in fourth grade and third grade, too, so he was used to being humongous. Somewhere along the line, he'd figured out that size was strength and strength was power.

So he charged admission to the playground.

If you wanted to play outside during recess, you had to pay him a quarter a week. This was back in the days when one play on a video game cost a quarter. It wasn't a lot of money, but it added up. And he was smart, too. He never got caught. Butch's rules were simple. If you didn't pay, you didn't play. And if you caused him trouble, he'd pound you into the dirt.

So we paid, and everything went on like normal, until my cousin, Adam Seigal, transferred into the school in late October.

When Adam heard about Butch's playground tax, he was outraged.

"I'm not going to pay that," he said, indignant. Adam was a skinny little guy with glasses. When he put down his foot, you had to laugh. "It's ridiculous. Somebody should tell the teachers."

"I think they know," I said. "I think Butch bribes them."

"Come on." He frowned. "Well, I'm not going to."

"What are you going to do?" I asked. "He'll grind you into hamburger."

Adam shrugged. "I just won't go on the playground."

He didn't, either. He stayed in the lunchroom or went to the library. If a teacher kicked him outside, Adam stayed close to the school building and sort of blended in with the bricks.

Adam managed to keep out of Butch's way until just after the winter holidays.

During the vacation break, Adam got a brand-new winter coat. It was a down-filled parka, big and warm and bright bright red. When he put it on, it made him look like a giant tomato with legs, arms, and a tiny head.

The first day back was cold but clear, and the principal shooed everybody outside.

Adam tried to hide, but Butch spotted him.

"Hey, you! Shrimp!" Butch's voice was like the low rumble of a school bus that's lost its muffler. "Where'd you come from?"

"Japan, Italy, Korea, Germany, Mexico, and most recently, Spain," Adam muttered. His father, my Uncle Peter, had been a translator for the army before finally retiring and opening up a gas station.

I don't think Butch heard. He roared, "C'mere! You owe me some money."

Fortunately, it was late in the period, and Adam was literally saved by the bell. It rang, and he raced inside.

After school, he ran home as fast as he could. He banged through the front door, dropped his coat in a heap, ignored his mother's shout of hello, and raced upstairs to the attic where our Great-Uncle Morris lived.

Adam knocked on the ceiling door and waited until he heard the faint, "All right already, come in." Then he lifted the trapdoor and climbed up.

The attic had a low roof, with one window at each end. There was a small bookshelf, a small television, a small card table with two chairs, and a twin bed.

Uncle Morris was sitting at the table, playing solitaire. He was a short man who always wore a tiny starched shirt and crisply pressed slacks, even when he was in his bathrobe. He was in his seventies at the time. When he felt good, he went for walks or swam at the Senior Center. When he was feeling poorly, he lowered a bucket down for his dinner and ate alone.

If you didn't know who he was, you'd probably think that Uncle Morris had made his living as a dapper garden gnome or one of Santa's elves in a high-priced department store.

The truth was that Uncle Morris used to be the world's smallest professional wrestler. He'd been billed as Mo the Midget and toured for years, mostly as a good guy. After four cups of wine on Passover, he'd brag that he'd never been thrown out of the ring unless he wanted to go. My dad said he once saw an amazing match where Uncle Morris flipped Sergeant Slaughter completely upside down.

Mo the Midget had done all right on the road, until wrestling started to be televised and the managers told him that his face was too ugly for the tube. He'd offered to wear a mask, but the answer was no. He was done. He left the show and traveled around the world for a few decades, spent most of his money, and came home at last, which was how he ended up living in my cousin's attic.

"You look worried, nephew," Uncle Morris said. He collected the cards into a neat pile, tapping the edges on the table. "You got a problem?"

Adam nodded and said, "When you were in the ring, how did you win?"

Uncle Morris sighed and carefully set the deck down on the table. "Did something happen?"

Adam shook his head. "Not yet. But I'm... Look, you fought against guys who were three or four times your size and you nearly always won. How did you do that?"

"Well, nephew," Uncle Morris hesitated, "you know professional wrestling is fixed, don't you? It's show biz. You can't fight two thousand rounds in a year for real. It would kill you. As it was it was brutal enough."

"So you didn't really win?" Adam's hopes shattered. "It was always a setup?"

"Well, no," Uncle Morris said indignantly, "I wouldn't go that far. I knew the moves. I had to. When you're out on tour, there's always a new guy, some punk who wants to prove himself. He's not willing to take a dive and look like an idiot against a little fella like me. Or some towns, they had these open matches when anybody from the audience could challenge anybody on the tour. That's when I had to know what I was doing. You bet."

The old man had a faraway look in his eye and a smile on his wrinkled cheeks.

After a moment, he spoke again. "You want to know the four secrets?"

Adam nodded, not daring to say a word.

"Okay." Uncle Morris said, holding up his right thumb. "Number one, relax."

He stuck out his index finger. "Number two, keep your distance. Get out of the way."

He stuck out his middle finger. "Number three, if you can, have a secret weapon."

He stuck out his ring finger. "Number four, show compassion."

He looked at his fingers, counted them, silently ran through the list again, nodded, and then closed his hand into a fist.

"That's it?" Adam said, his voice squeaking a little.

"Hey, it worked for me. If I was ten years younger and you had a month, I'd train you, but a little theory with no technique is better than a little technique with no theory. Now, how about a game of cribbage?"

Adam relaxed while they played, but that night he went to bed praying for snow.

It didn't snow.

The next day, in the lunchroom, Butch spotted Adam, pointed his fingers like a gun, and mouthed, "I'm gonna get you, shrimp."

My cousin could barely finish his lunch.

As far as I was concerned, it was amazing that Adam ever finished his lunches. When they'd lived abroad, his mom had liked to cook local gourmet foods. She'd taken pride in seeking out the most obscure dishes of the region. As a result, Adam always had the weirdest and most disgusting leftovers you could possibly imagine. He brought stuff like calamari, blood sausage, or cabrito, which was a spicy goat's-head stew.

On this particular day, his mom had packed a liverwurst and wasabi sandwich on black bread, with a slice of onion and a slathering of incredibly foul-smelling kimchi. And he'd washed it all down with a purple cow — a blend of whole milk and Coke.

I don't know how he even walked after a meal like that, let alone shrugged into his tomato coat and shuffled out of the cafeteria into the bright January sunshine.

Butch was waiting. "You gonna pay your toll?" he rasped.

Adam shook his head.

"What?" Butch bellowed, edging closer.

A crowd of kids quickly gathered.

"I said no. No, I'm not going to pay you."

The crowd gasped. I wanted to shout to Adam, "Stop being a fool and give the bully a quarter!" Everybody was watching, and in just a little while I'd have to scrape my cousin off the blacktop.

"You're not going to pay?" Butch shouted, smiling at all the kids. "Then I guess I'll have to squeeze it out of you."

And without any warning, as quick as a rattlesnake, Butch grabbed Adam in a bear hug and started to squeeze.

Adam's face went wild with fear and pain. He hadn't been paying attention. Butch held him tight. Adam struggled and squirmed. His eyes began to pop, so he shut them.

That's when Uncle Morris' words came back to him.

"Number one, relax."

So he did. He went limp and slid right out of his bright red down jacket. He dropped to the ground, rolled away, and left Butch standing in the middle of the playground squeezing the life out of an empty coat.

"Wha—?" Butch sputtered. "Hey, where'd he go?"

"I am not paying," Adam said defiantly. He bounced back and forth on the tips of his toes, as if he desperately needed to go to the bathroom.

Butch looked at him. "I'm gonna get you." Then he charged like a wild animal.

Rule number two, Uncle Morris had said, was "Keep your distance. Get out of the way."

Adam turned around and ran like the wind. Butch stayed on his tail. Adam broke through the crowd and ran out onto the field, touching playground dirt for the first time since he'd transferred to Fernwood. A cheer went up as Butch lumbered after him.

They looped out around the kindergarten play set, through the empty soccer goal posts, and raced back toward the blacktop.

Adam was still safely ahead, breathing hard, but not as hard as Butch. Butch sounded like he was going to die. Panting and shouting, "I'm. Gonna. Get. You. Shrimp."

If he hadn't gotten overconfident, Adam could have stayed away from Butch all afternoon. He was small and in shape. Butch was big and slow.

Adam waved as he ran back into the circle of schoolchildren, grabbed up his coat, and stopped dead.

"Keep going!" I yelled. "He's coming!"

Adam shook his head. He had other plans.

Butch pushed through the kids, nearly stumbled, and then stopped. He glared at Adam.

Adam smiled back. He held his jacket in front of him. He waved it like a matador's cape. That's when I remembered that my cousin had spent a year in Madrid.

"Toro!" Adam shouted. "Toro!"

Butch snorted, curled his lips, and with his arms in front of him charged.

If Butch had been a bull, Adam would have dodged him quite nimbly.

Unfortunately for Adam, as soon as Butch got close enough, he opened his arms wide and snatched at Adam and his coat. He snagged Adam's wrist, held on tight, and spun my cousin back into his bear hug.

"You're dead now, shrimp," Butch panted, trying to catch his breath. The crowd was invisible. There was only Butch and the bug who had dared defy him. A bug he would crush in a minute.

Adam's breath went out of him. His stomach pushed in. His face went red. His lips began to flutter.

Then it happened. We all saw it.

Adam burped — and it came out green. You could see it! We all watched as these wavy droplets of moisture floated in the chilly playground air like moldy steam, and blew right into Butch's face.

The mist reached Butch just as he was inhaling. He snorted the fetid fumes from Adam's partially digested lunch up his nose and into his lungs.

Butch dropped Adam, stumbled and fell back, coughing, hacking. He fell to one knee and stared at my cousin, who was sitting on the ground like a pile of dirty laundry.

"You're disgusting," Butch said, shaking his head.

Adam tried to grin, but it looked like a grimace of pain.

"Get away from me," Butch said, rising shakily. "Just get away."

That's when I heard somebody jeer, "The shrimp beat the bully. The shrimp beat the bully."

I wish I'd started it, but I took it up, and it quickly spread. You know that schoolyard cadence. It's a horrible teasing singsong tune. "The shrimp beat the bully."

"He did not," Butch said. "I'm letting him go."

Now we were all shouting together. "The shrimp beat the bully." All of us were united at last against Butch. "The shrimp beat the bully!"

Butch was screaming now, yelling at the top of his lungs. "No, he didn't. He's disgusting, that's all. Cut it out!"

But we didn't. We kept going. Over and over and over again, until a shrill two-finger-in-mouth whistle, stopped us cold.

It was Adam. He took his fingers out of his mouth. "Hey," he said. "Don't say that." He was standing beside Butch. "Don't say that about my friend Butch."

"Huh?" Butch looked puzzled.

Adam stared out at us, both feet planted firmly on the blacktop. "Don't you guys say that about my friend Butch."

We were as stunned as Butch. Nobody said a word. There was dead silence on the playground.

"You know what Butch told me? He said that he's going to stop charging admission to the playground."

"I did?" Butch said.

A cheer went up.

"I did," Butch admitted, lying.

"In fact," Adam continued, "my friend Butch said he's going to give all the money back."

Even more cheers filled the yard. Hats and bookbags went flying through the air. It was quite a celebration.

"Uh, Adam," Butch mumbled, "I spent all the money."

"Oh. Okay, okay," Adam quickly said. "Guys, I was wrong. Butch says he can't give the money back, but he's still sorry, right?"

Butch nodded.

We all booed.

"Stop it!" Adam shouted. "Stop making fun of my friend Butch."

And we stopped. It was the strangest thing.

Butch looked at Adam and stuck out his hand. They shook.

We stared at the two of them standing together, and even before the bell rang, everyone started to wander off.

Later on, I asked Adam what the heck he was thinking.

He told me. "Rule number one, relax. Rule number two, maintain your distance and get out of the way.

Rule number three, have a secret weapon. Rule number four, show compassion."

I nodded, not really understanding. I'm not sure what would have happened if Adam hadn't managed that vile belch, but I'm not sure I care.

You see, for the rest of the year, everyone played on the playground in peace, and for free. And after that, Adam and Butch really were best of friends.

Runninghead

WHEN I was a kid we used to scare each other with stories about it. It was the kind of thing that the big kids inflicted on the little kids and the little kids inflicted on their littler brothers and sisters. Of course I heard about it from Ellen, but I also heard about it from my best friend, David Kovar. And after my cousin Adam moved to town, he heard about it too.

Runninghead.

Some said that it was the skull of a murdered jogger. They said that it ran around the high school track after dark on every full moon.

Others claimed that it was the long-haired skull of a mother who had just left her babies at home for a moment to go out for liquor and cigarettes and had driven her car into the Breakneck River Canal. She went through the windshield, back before safety glass, and her spine severed in several places. Even though she was dead on impact, she had to get back to her children before anything horrible happened, so she assembled the pieces as quickly as she could, leaving out part of the middle and began running home.

Still others believed it was just a deformed head with legs. They said it was a giant head on normal size legs, like one of those Easter Island statues, but without the body in between.

Everyone said a lot of different things.

And when you were a kid, you believed a lot of those. Maybe all of them. I mean, why wouldn't you? People were supposed to tell the truth. They weren't supposed to make up scary stories just to scare the pants off little kids, were they?

But after a while, you started to realize that maybe it wasn't so likely that a jaw bone would sit on top of a pair of thighs and haul its abbreviated carcass through dark and deserted streets without once getting caught by the cops, a newspaper reporter, or being clipped by a passing truck.

The first time I stopped believing was the time that I told what I knew about the story to Adam. He'd asked me to fill him in on the details and when I told him what I remembered, and I saw that he still needed more, I kept going. I embellished. I made stuff up just to scare him.

I told him that one story was that Runninghead was a golfer whose ball landed in the middle of the train tracks and, rather than take a penalty stroke, he decided to play it where it lay. His foot got caught between the rails and the ties, and the train was coming fast. He thwacked the ball just as the cowcatcher caught him. The ball landed right in the hole for a birdie and rather than just laying down and dying, the golfer picked himself up, rolled his head on top of his pants, tightened his belt and raced back to his foursome, all of whom met tragic endings.

I took great pleasure in whispering those words, "all of whom met tragic endings." When Adam pushed me for more details about those tragic endings, I sidestepped by talking about Runninghead's bloodied lime green trousers and spiked shoes with those funky tasseled laces.

Adam's eyes widened in amazement, and I realized that I'd completely hooked him. If I'd wanted to, I could have told him stories that would have kept him up for a month. To be honest, I thought about it, but then I thought about what my Aunt Dorothy would do to me if I kept going, and I decided that it wasn't worth it.

"Of course I don't believe in Runninghead," I told Adam with a bit of a scoff.

I was wrong.

It was summertime, the night of a full moon, and I was biking home from a late night session of Diplomacy at David Kovar's.

When I was a kid, everybody biked everywhere all the time. We were too young to have cars, but nobody minded. You could get around pretty far and pretty fast with two wheels and two legs. We didn't wear helmets back then, because nobody knew how dangerous head injuries were, and we didn't have flashing halogen LED taillights because they hadn't been invented yet. After dark, we biked in the dark, and kept our eyes open for parked cars full of teenagers and swerving cars full of inebriated adults. Nobody I knew ever got killed or even injured, except my friend Joel who was clotheslined by a car door that suddenly opened in front of him. And that was in broad daylight on a busy street. He was fine. I guess we were all lucky.

Diplomacy is this old-fashioned semi-board game that's all about conquering the world by negotiation, backstabbing, and lying. It's sort of a primer for world politics. We were a bunch of dorky guys who liked pretending we were international leaders, and the sessions got pretty heated and lasted hours without much real progress or change. (Which I guess was another lesson about the way the world really worked.) We made huge bowls of popcorn, drank gallons of caffeinated soda, and aside from waking up Kovar's baby brother with our shouting, stayed out of trouble.

About quarter to twelve, David's mother broke up the party. She'd called our parents and said we were on our way. We all shook hands and promised to meet again next week.

While I wheeled my bike out from behind David's garage, he said, "You better watch out."

"I'll be careful."

"No," he said. "It's a full moon." He nodded up at the sky.

The moon was high and bright. It was like a giant glowing white beach ball. The man in the moon looked like an old-fashioned newspaper cartoon, grinning and wild-eyed.

"Yeah, it's bright," I said, throwing my leg over the bar and sliding into my saddle. "Easier to see things."

"It's almost midnight," David said. "You're going to be rolling by the graveyard at midnight on the night of a full moon."

"What you're thinking, ghosts?"

He shook his head. "Naw. Runninghead."

"Runninghead?"

Now he nodded. "Yep."

"You trying to scare me?" I said.

He nodded. "Yeah, I am. I know you don't believe in Runninghead, but it's real. That cemetery? Night of a full moon? Runninghead. I'd be worried."

"Well," I shrugged. "Not me. See you tomorrow at the swimming pool."

And I pedaled off. I wasn't afraid. Really. I wasn't.

Not at first.

You know how somebody's words get inside your brain whether you want them to or not. They say something, and you kind of blow them off, but the words stick, and they begin to spin around and around. Over and over. Repeating themselves like a mental version of the Chinese water torture. Drip. Drip. Drip.

David's words were zipping through my brain.

Full moon. Cemetery. Runninghead.

Now I need to give you a little geographical description of my town. It was a pretty ordinary place. I lived on one side, and David lived on the other. In the old days you'd call his neighborhood the other side of the tracks, but the property values had gone up and there were really no poor sections. We had a little downtown with a public library, city hall, police station, hospital, businesses, science museum and so on.

For me to get to David's house, I had to bike through my neighborhood, through downtown, up Steeple Hill, past the old churchyard, zip down Steeple Hill, over the train tracks, around the graveyard, and then through his neighborhood to his house. In a car it was ten minutes. On a bike, if you were going fast it was about twenty-five minutes because of the hill, which was gigantic. Every big snowstorm some crazy kid got hurt because he sledded too far and too fast and hit a tree. We all kept doing it because it was a lot of fun. I knew, because I'd gotten creamed there twice.

Getting back home from David's house was the same thing in reverse. You really couldn't go any other way because the Breakneck River Canal was on one side of town and the prison was on the other.

The light from the moon was a beacon in my eyes as I started pedaling through David's neighborhood.

I'm not afraid, I said. I'm cool.

Then, up ahead, I saw the graveyard.

Our town was pretty old, and the graveyard was original. It went back to the seventeen-hundreds, and all of the founders and their children and grandchildren were buried there. It had Civil War veterans and almost everybody else who died and wasn't buried in some churchyard or another. In daylight sometimes, weird ladies went around and made charcoal rubbings of the grave markers. At night it had the usual amount of spooky goofy party stuff that any place like that attracts. The wrought iron fence was high and pointy, but there were enough places where the bars were down that if you wanted to squeeze your way in you could.

Or if something wanted to squeeze its way out.

Cemetery. Full moon…

I sat up and, pedaling no hands, pushed the button on my digital watch. The red LED numbers blinked on.

11:59

I wasn't afraid. It was one of those suburban myths. A spooky story that they told Boy Scouts to give them a thrill.

Nevertheless it wouldn't hurt to pick up the pace.

I was rolling at a pretty good speed when I took the right turn to go around the far side of the graveyard toward the train tracks.

Fast enough that I almost didn't hear the sounds.

A creak. And a thump. And then footsteps.

My heart was already racing, but that was just the energy I was using to bike. Right? It was my imagination.

Cemetery. Graveyard. Full Moon. Midnight.

I pulled my hands off the handlebars fast enough to activate the watch again.

12:00

Runninghead.

My heart was pounding faster, but it was nothing. There was nothing following me. It was not happening. I wasn't going to look back. Why waste the energy?

As Satchel Paige once said, "Don't look back, something might be gaining on you."

I looked back.

There was nothing there. I gasped with relief. I didn't see anything. There really was nothing there. My shoulders heaved as the tension began to release. I slowed my pedaling.

And that's when I heard the footsteps again. Coming closer and closer.

Rapid slapping footsteps.

It was like the whap-whap-whap-whap of a wet fish being splattered on the sidewalk.

It didn't sound like a person. When a human being runs there's a rhythm, but it's irregular. There are breaks in the motion from dodging obstacles or adjusting for terrain.

This sound was relentless. The rhythm was regular, like there was something stuck in a piece of damp machinery thwacking against something solid.

Runninghead? Graveyard. Full moon. Midnight. No way.

I looked back again and I almost fell off my bike.

It was a gigantic head the size of a medicine ball with two gigantic eyes, big and bloodshot red. You could see them glaring in the moonlight. It had no nose, just a flat spot with two holes where the nose should be. And it had a gigantic gaping mouth with big white sharp teeth, the kind you see on crocodiles or in a shark's maw. The jaw was opening and closing, clicking and clacking, and this long purple tongue was slathering in and out and licking spittle and drool between chomps.

Beneath the head were two of the tiniest feet I had ever seen, but they were moving like blurs on skinny bird legs.

I hit a bump in the road, which was a good thing, because it woke me up.

Whether this was real or not, I needed to get home. So I turned my face firmly forward and started to ride.

Pat-spat pat-splat pat-spat …

I shouldn't have slowed down. Maybe it wouldn't have chased me if I hadn't shown any weakness. I gave myself some energy and pushed harder.

Pat-pat-pat-pat-patpatpatpat... It was speeding up too.

I grabbed my handlebars tighter and felt my knuckles go white. I stood on the pedals, bent my knees, and hit the train tracks faster than recommended speed.

Ba-doum ba-doum badoum-badoum.

My arms were jolted as I rolled over the rails.

I looked back. It was still there. I had gained a little bit of distance, but watched in horror as it jumped the steel rails like an Olympic hurdler from Munchkin Land.

Pat-spat leap! Pat-splat leap!

This was freaking me out. I stayed standing and began to run on my bike.

That's when I saw Steeple Hill right in front of me, like Mount Everest, or a wall. It might as well have been.

I was already out of breath. There was something on my tail, and whether it was real or not I didn't care. I had to get up the highest hill in the world at midnight with a full moon shining and this thing chasing after me.

People say that human beings are capable of amazing feats of strength. They talk about mothers lifting cars off their babies. They talk about lost boys walking for months across deserts.

They don't talk about what happens when you run out of steam and know you're going to die. My heart was pounding. My lungs were aching. I couldn't feel my toes as I pushed my legs left and right.

Pat-spat. It was louder. I didn't look back. It was gaining.

I couldn't stand any taller. I couldn't move any faster. The hill was getting steeper and steeper. I was in the easiest gear on my bike and I was barely moving.

It would have been faster to get off and run.

Pat-splat.

But getting off my bike would have taken time, and if I slowed down or fell, I might never get back on… And then I remembered.

Steeple Hill was a tall hill in all directions. That's why they built the church up there, so that it would be the highest building that anyone could see. When I got to the top, if I got to the top, once I was past the church, it was downhill.

PAT-SPAT. PAT SPLAT chomp-SLURP.

The mind is an amazing motivator. Combine the disgusting sounds of those tiny feet, the clacking teeth, and that purple tongue with my realization that I might actually be able to get away.

My legs went faster. Beyond cramp and pain to this place where I felt like I was pushing pistons.

The bike kept moving. I crested the top of Steeple Hill, shifted into another gear, and kept pushing past the churchyard.

For a brief moment I hoped that some savior-like deity would come out and expunge this evil thing from the world.

Didn't happen.

It was past the churchyard, and it was still coming after me. I could hear it. I glanced back and it was closer. It was bigger. Its teeth were glittering in the moonlight.

I pumped and pumped, gathering speed, hooked over the top of the hill, shifted into my hardest gear, pumped and pumped again as gravity grabbed me and started to pull.

You add thirty-two feet per second squared to the force of terror and you get a lot of speed. I was moving fast. I crouched low over my handlebars and felt the wind on my face. I was a human boy on wheels and that thing only had little stubby feet. No way it was going to get me.

The rumbling noise started slowly. I thought it was thunder at first, but the sky was clear and cloud-free. I didn't see any lightning.

I looked back and the head was rolling. It had retracted its feet and was rolling like a boulder down the side of a mountain.

They say that objects fall at the same rate, so that my rolling and its rolling should have kept us the same distance apart, but it was gaining on me. Maybe it was lubricating its slide with its tongue. I don't know.

I tried to pedal faster but my gears couldn't catch up with the speed of my flywheel.

It was getting closer and there was nothing I could do.

I was watching the ground. The bottom of the hill was dead ahead. It was like looking at the bottom of a cliff. We were almost there. I was out of steam. I was out of energy. I was out of ideas.

It was breathing hard with anticipation and hunger. I could smell the fetid odor of its rotting breath. In the corner of my eye I saw sparks flying behind me as its chattering teeth chipped off pieces of the concrete road.

I was never going to see my parents again. Kovar was going to feel really lousy when he read about me in the papers. Ellen I didn't care so much about, because she'd probably convince my parents to knock a hole through our bedroom walls so she could make my room into another closet for all her clothes.

I hit the bottom of the hill with a jolt.

I looked up and saw the science museum looming in front of me.

I didn't think; I banked.

I turned sharply right, bounced the curb in front of the science museum, wobbled, but didn't lose control.

Newton said that a body in motion tends to stay in motion unless acted upon by an external force. This thing didn't have a body, but it also didn't have a steering wheel.

The Runninghead went straight. It popped over the curb, rolled right up the steps, and slammed through the front door of the science museum, breaking the old wood like a battering ram through Popsicle sticks.

I didn't wait around to see if it was going to come after me. I booked home. I don't even remember the rest of the ride. I dropped my bike in the driveway, ran into the house, locked the door, ran to my room, locked my door, jumped into bed, and pulled the covers over my head.

And then it was morning.

Mom was making pancakes for breakfast.

On the front page of the newspaper was the headline, “Vandals Wreck Museum.”

The lead paragraphs read, “Last night, shortly after midnight, unknown vandals broke into the science museum, trashing exhibits, wreaking havoc and completely destroying Old Buckwheat, the beloved stuffed Civil War horse that has served as unoffical mascot of the city, and a favorite of children for so many years. Inquiries are still proceeding, but the police currently have no clues.”

When my Dad came in to yell at me because he’d nearly backed the car over my bike, I ran over to him and gave him a big hug.

Which left him very confused.

At the pool, when Kovar asked how was the ride, I told him. He said I was making it up. I wasn’t.

After that, when I biked to and from Kovar’s, I went blocks out of my way to keep distance from that cemetery. And if the moon was full, I slept over.

Middleduction

MOST AUTHORS start or finish with their own thoughts. Personally, I don't like to slog through either introductions or afterwords. I wanted you, kind reader, to begin with "It Ate My Sister" and finish with "Ellen vs. the Snakes" because they bookend this collection so nicely. I find prefaces disingenuous, and by the time I'm done with the book, if the author has something else to say, an afterword often seems gratuitous.

Of course maybe nothing is more gratuitous than to interrupt the flow of stories with a bit of self-indulgent explanation. Consider this akin to the color-commentary during the halftime show at the Super Bowl. (Or not, since the commercials are now much more impressive than the show itself.)

Critics and English teachers often look for the meaning, morals, and messages in my stories. They ask about character development, growth, and change. They want to know why a story was written or what its true purpose is. I usually sidestep the question by asking them, "What do you think?" Whatever answer they give, I smile and nod knowingly, as if agreeing that they are certainly correct.

Readers and listeners often ask if my stories are true. I typically joke back, "All my stories are true and some of them really happened." This is what I call the "Politician's Answer." It's neither a lie nor the truth, but passes the time long enough for the focus to shift to a better topic.

Nevertheless, in an era where reality television isn't considered an oxymoron, I think it's worthwhile to address the issue of veracity just a bit. Any discerning reader can figure out which elements in these stories are "true" and which are exaggerations. You are a discerning reader, insomuch as you've made it this far and haven't hurled the book across the room (or hit the delete button if you're reading this on some electronic doohickey). Therefore, you already know what's true and what is patently false. In other words, I'm going to pass the buck and tell you something my father once said to me when I was bugging him with questions about a movie we were watching together.

"If you can't figure out what's going on, then I'm not going to tell you. Be quiet and stop hogging the popcorn."

It was frustrating and annoying even then.

As for the hidden meaning or deeper purpose behind this collection… With any luck, some day, Ellen's kids will ask her, "Mom, did that really happen?" And they won't believe her no matter what she says.

Where There's Smoke…

WE WEREN'T very religious when I was growing up, but every Friday night was "Family Night." We'd light candles, eat braided challah bread, and say the blessing over the wine. It was fine when we were younger, but when Ellen, my older sister, reached a certain age, I took to calling it the blessing over the whining.

"Why do I have to stay home on Friday night?" she always complained. "Everybody else is going out."

To which my mother answered, as mothers always will, "If everybody else was jumping off a bridge would you?"

Ellen just glared.

I didn't mind. Nobody asks a younger brother out on a Friday night. Still, it was fun to watch Ellen squirm and pout.

Then, one day in late April, my father announced, "We're all going out next Friday night."

"Not to shul," Ellen whined. "Please. Ever since Rabbi Glotnick died it's been so boring."

"Ellen!" said my mother, shocked that she'd even say such a thing — because it was true. Our synagogue used to have a brilliant, witty, and entertaining rabbi. Rabbi Isaac Glotnick was known in our town as the wacky and fun religious guy. He died of a sudden heart attack. Now, Rabbi Glazer, the old retired rabbi emeritus, was pinch-hitting until the search committee came up with a replacement. My cousin, Adam, joked it was like the difference between nighttime baseball with lights, and nighttime baseball without lights. Where once everyone had laughed and sang, now everyone snored.

Nevertheless, to say so was the height of rudeness.

Fortunately, that wasn't what Dad had planned.

"Next week," he said, "Friday night is Lag B'Omer, and we are going camping."

That stopped the conversation cold.

"What?" said Mom. What she really meant was, "Have you lost your mind?"

"Camping?" said Ellen.

Dad nodded. "Lag B'Omer is this holiday I heard about where you're supposed to light a bonfire. I thought it would be fun."

"Cool," said I.

"Yep," said Dad. "I've already talked to the Joneses, and we're going to borrow their camper."

"Honey," Mom said, clearly relieved, "why didn't you say so?"

Our next-door neighbors were the Joneses. You know, as in the Keeping-Up-With-The Joneses. They had everything. They had a swimming pool, the first color TV, the first video games, and the first Winnebago with a stove, waterbed, bunk beds, toilet, and wet bar. It was like a swinging bachelor pad on wheels.

But that Friday, when Dad came home from work early, he didn't drive up in the Winnebago. Instead, he'd borrowed the Joneses old car-camper trailer. It looked like a big flat gift box on two wheels, only brown with white stripes. You tow it behind your car, and when you get to the campground, you crank it up and it turns into a tent.

"We're going camping in this?" Mom said. (Again meaning, "Are you insane?") "Is there a stove?"

Dad put his arm around her. "We're going to build a campfire. It wouldn't be camping otherwise. A big campfire. Why, it's practically a commandment for the holiday!"

Ellen rolled her eyes. Me, I was psyched. I was of the age where burning things was both fun and cool. I liked melting toy soldiers and torching old model tanks. A bonfire was way up on my list of things to do.

To her credit, Mom sucked it up, and started packing. Two hours later we were off, heading to a lakeside campground in the Berkshires my Dad had heard about from the Joneses, singing "She'll be coming round the mountain," loudly and off key.

We pulled off the highway onto a dirt road. We pulled off the dirt road onto a narrower dirt road. We turned off the narrower dirt road onto a skinny dirt road that was really nothing more than a trail with a couple of ruts. By then, it was getting dark.

"Okay kids," Dad said, "Watch this."

Dad turned off the headlights. All of a sudden, it got real dark.

Mom screeched, "What are you doing!"

"I'm driving without the lights on," Dad said. "Isn't it amazing what you can see in the dark? Kids, this is how the Indians traveled after dark. They didn't have lights."

"They didn't have cars either," Ellen said. Her fingers were gripping the door handle, as if she was getting ready to jump.

"Stop the car," Mom said.

"We're almost there," Dad replied. "It's just down this hill."

"Stop the car. Or turn on the lights."

"In a sec. See, the road's getting smoother..."

"STOP THE CAR!" Mom screamed.

Dad slammed on the brakes. We all bounced forward. If we'd had air bags in those days, they would have exploded.

"Okay kids," Dad said, "we're here. See, it's fine."

Dad turned on the headlights. They were under water. The front of the car was under water.

We'd found the campsite, and we'd also found the boat ramp. In fact, we'd nearly driven all the way down the boat ramp.

"I told you," Mom said, quietly.

Ellen leapt out, and scrambled away from the car. She sat on the campsite's picnic table, shaking her head.

"Ellen, shut the door," Dad said, as calmly as he could. "I'm going to back this up..."

My father had never backed up a trailer in his life. It jackknifed immediately. Dad started cursing.

"I guess we're here," Mom said. She turned to me. "Why don't you and your sister go out and gather some firewood while your father puts up the tent?"

It was clear that she wanted to talk to him in private, so we started searching. It's not easy finding firewood in the dark. We'd only brought the one flashlight, and Mom needed to hold it so Dad could see the tent. Nevertheless, Ellen and I stumbled around in the woods. Ellen was wondering if there were snakes. I was wondering about poison ivy. I kept telling her to watch out for the snakes and she kept telling me to watch out for poison ivy. She yelled at me, and I yelled back at her. My father yelled at both us to shut up and enjoy the silence, and then went back to cursing the tent.

Eventually, we scavenged a few dry logs, and piled them in the middle of the campfire circle. I tried to start the fire by rubbing two sticks together. I'd read about it, like every other kid who dreams about starting fires. After fifteen minutes of struggle, Ellen pushed me aside.

"Here," she said in exasperation, "let me do that."

Two seconds later, the fire was roaring.

"Whoah!" I said. "How'd you do that?"

"Matches," she said, waving a pack, which she then stuffed into her jeans pocket.

"Honey," Mom said. "Why don't you take a break and let's light the Sabbath candles and eat some supper?"

"Fine." Dad threw down the crank.

Mom had set the picnic table with plates, forks, napkins, candles, cups, challah, and a Kiddush cup. She tried to light the candles, but the wind kept blowing them out. Finally, she gave up and said the blessing over the campfire.

"It'll have to do," she explained.

Dinner was hot dogs, cole slaw, and potato chips. We stuck the dogs on sticks and roasted them over the fire. Instead of buns we used slices of challah. It was delicious. Roasted marshmallows for dessert. We sat and laughed and watched the flickering flames for a long time.

At last, it was time to go to bed. By then, it had gotten fairly cold, and we were looking forward to our sleeping bags.

Unfortunately, Dad still hadn't gotten the tent all the way up. Or rather he'd managed to get it halfway up. One part of the tent was open, and the other part was partly open, so it looked like a Frank Lloyd Wright house. Or maybe a Frank Lloyd Wrong house.

"That's the best I can do," he said. "At least we'll be out of the wind."

Shaking her head, Mom took the flashlight, and opened the camper's door. She stopped cold.

"Spiders," she said, softly.

"What?" Dad asked.

"Spiders." Her voice was little more than a whisper.

Dad sighed. "Oh, come on. A little spider is not going to..."

"You come here," Mom hissed. She handed him the flashlight. "Look."

Dad shined the flashlight into the camper, and paled. He started to sweat and his face turned white, like someone had smeared mayonnaise over it. "Holy..."

I ran over and looked inside. There weren't just a few little spiders. There was webbing everywhere and the entire inside of the camper was crawling with hundreds, if not thousands, of spiders of all shapes and sizes. "Whoah!" I said, "Cool."

Dad jumped back as the spiders started to pour out the door. "Ahh!" He slammed the door shut. His teeth were chattering.

Mom heaved a sigh the size of a boulder. "We'll just have to sleep in the car."

"Why can't we go back home?" Ellen asked.

"Because we're never going to be able to close up the camper and back out of here until daylight," Mom said, sensibly.

"That's it!" Ellen yelped, "this family is crazy." And she took off into the woods.

"Don't go far," Mom called after her. "Bedtime in half an hour."

Mom fixed Dad a cup of instant coffee, and soon his hands stopped shaking. Then she got our sleeping bags out of the trunk.

"I wanted this to be a nice celebration. You know, a family ritual."

"Yes dear," Mom said, patting him on the shoulder. She looked at me. "Go get your sister."

I could see she wanted a little more time alone with Dad, so I left them and hiked off in the direction Ellen had gone.

This time, I practiced walking like an Indian, silently. I was hoping to sneak up on her, yell, "BOO!" and watch her jump out of her skin.

Then I smelled the smoke, and I panicked. I was worried that we'd accidentally started a fire, and that my sister might get burned, so I just ran blindly ahead.

She did look startled. She was in a clearing, sitting on a big rock. She looked guilty too, and it only took me a moment to figure out why. By the light of the stars I could see that she was busily grinding a cigarette butt out against the boulder.

"You're smoking," I said.

"Duh," she answered. She didn't even deny it.

"Mom and Dad'll kill you," I said. "How long have you been smoking.

"Not if you don't tell them," she said, a threatening tone in her voice. "It's none of your business."

"It is too," I said. "Uncle Sid died of lung cancer. He had one of those tracheotomies. You remember. It was disgusting. I'm going to tell them. Mom! Dad!"

"Shut up, creep," Ellen said, hissing. "What'll it take to keep you quiet?"

"You give me the cigarettes and promise to stop smoking, and I won't tell them."

We heard Mom calling, "Is everything okay?"

I held out my hand.

Ellen grudgingly dropped the pack in my palm.

"Everything's fine," I yelled back. "I was just checking."

Ellen shook her head in rage and started walking back to the campground. I shoved the pack in my pocket, and hurried after her.

It was a miserable night in the car. Nobody was comfortable. Dad snored and Mom farted. By morning we were all miserable and cranky. I was the first awake. I don't even know if I slept. The car windows were completely steamed up, so you couldn't see a thing.

"I've got to get out of here," I said, yanking open the car door at the first hint of dawn.

"Shut the door!" everybody else yelled. So I slammed it shut.

It was awesome outside. The sun was just coming up over the far end of the lake, brushing its rosy fingers over the layer of mist floating above the water. Some birds were hooting off in the distance. Other than that, it was quiet.

I felt at peace.

For about two minutes.

Then Ellen came out and slammed her car door and plopped down next to me.

"Mom farted again," she said.

I nodded, still looking out across the lake.

"Bet you won't go for a swim." she said.

"Bet I will."

"Bet you won't."

"Double dare?"

"Triple," she grinned.

Then I did one of the stupidest things ever. I ran, fully dressed into a mountain lake in early May.

The water was so cold it felt like somebody had poured ice into my shoes.

I screeched, slipped on the slick slimed-covered boat ramp, and fell all the way under.

It was so cold I could barely breathe.

A moment later, I popped up, gasping and shivering.

By then my parents were out of the car and racing for the lake.

Dad grabbed a long stick and held it out to me. I snagged it, and he tugged me in to shore.

"You poor dear," Mom said. "Let's get you out of those."

I was shivering, so she stripped me naked and stuffed me into my sleeping bag and poured me into the car.

The shivering stopped, and I started to feel warm.

Then Mom knocked on the car window. "Are you okay? Good. Can you come out here? Now."

I nodded, and then bunny-hopped out in my sleeping bag. Mom and Dad were sitting on the picnic bench, looking concerned. Ellen was watching.

"What are these?" Mom asked. She held out her hand and I saw a soggy, crumpled pack of cigarettes.

For a moment I wasn't sure what was going on. "Cigarettes," I said, honestly.

"'Cigarettes,' he says," Mom echoed.

"Are these yours?" Dad asked, his voice deadly serious.

That's when I remembered. That's when I realized.

"No," I said, "They're..." I looked over at Ellen. She was stone still.

"They're not mine."

"They're not yours?" Mom demanded, clearly not believing me.

"No. They're not mine. I don't smoke. It's disgusting. I remember what happened to Uncle Sid. Gross."

"Where did you get them?" She insisted.

"I found them."

"You found them?"

"What is this, an echo?"

"Don't talk back," Dad said. "Where did you find them?"

I glanced at Ellen. Her face was rigid. She was holding her breath.

"I found them in the woods. Near a rock. I picked them up and put them in my pocket. I didn't want to litter."

There was a pause, and then I added, "Okay?"

"No, it is not okay," my Mom started, but she didn't know what else to say.

Ellen sighed. "Listen," she began.

My Dad interrupted. "Hey," he said. "It's okay. Enough's enough. This whole trip has been a disaster. At least one of us is cleaning up the mess."

Then he put his hand on my shoulder and said, "Thanks, son. You're a good kid."

My Mom looked at me, still not sure, and then she too nodded. "Okay. Fine. Don't scare me like that again."

"Go get dressed. Let's get packed up," Dad said. "I'm hungry and I don't want to stay here any longer than we have to."

And it was over. I put on a set of dry clothes. As quickly as that. Dad attacked the camper and wrestled it back into its box. Mom, Ellen and I repacked the car's trunk. Everybody helped unhitch the trailer, and then rehitch it, after Dad backed the car out of the lake.

Sometime during all this Ellen sneaked over next to me and whispered, "Thanks, creep."

"You're welcome," I said. "Remember, you promised to quit smoking."

She nodded, and I knew she would keep her word.

At last, everything was loaded and put away, and we headed down the mountain to civilization.

"Anyone up for the International House of Pancakes?" Dad said, followed by a round of cheers.

I had a double stack of buttermilk pancakes with blueberry syrup, and slept all the way back to our house.

The Tale of Bad Breath Bill

When my Uncle Morris told me this story, I thought for sure that he stole parts of it from "The Bully and the Shrimp." He, however, claimed it must be a case of thematic convergence. He swore it was something he'd heard about during his wrestling days when he was performing out in the foothills of the Medicine Bow Mountain Range in Wyoming...

ONCE UPON a time, in the far-ago days of the West, there was a cowboy who had breath so bad he could knock a mockingbird off the top of a ponderosa pine a hundred yards away. His name was Bad Breath Bill, but most of the other cowboys just called him Stinky.

Now, Stinky had been like that all his life. When he was born, he looked like just about any other child. But when the doctor spanked him on the behind, and Stinky started bawling, everybody in the room smelled a very peculiar odor, and immediately passed out cold. Fortunately, the doctor was holding Stinky right over his mother at the time, so he just dropped on her soft belly and fell asleep with the rest of them.

His mother called him William, but the name never stuck. Everyone else called him Stinky. They couldn't help themselves.

As Stinky grew up, his halitosis continued to be a problem. Most of the other children didn't want to play with him, and they'd tease him something fierce. They said (even though it wasn't true) that he could light fires with a sneeze, and that if he forgot to brush his teeth in the morning he could kill a cow just by blowing out of one nostril.

In the one-room school, the teachers had to put Stinky in the back next to the window, and they gave him a special tube to breath into. The tube went out the window, and if you followed it behind the school you'd see that all of the flowers and grass back there were black and dead.

The teachers tried to find a special kind of chalk for him, because when it was Stinky's turn to do a lesson on the board, the normal kind of chalk would melt from the smell, and all the letters would run like watercolor paint left out in the rain.

Now, it was just natural for Stinky to become a cowboy. His momma wanted him to become a banker, but whenever he went into the local Wells Fargo Bank to deposit his allowance, half of the customers closed out their accounts. She took him to doctors and she took him to dentists. Nothing ever came of it, except big bills and a shortage of qualified physicians and teeth pullers in the county. She took him to medicine men and medicine shows. Nothing helped.

Finally, when everybody else in town was sleeping, she took Stinky to see a veterinarian. She didn't want the schoolchildren to have anything else to tease him about, but she needed to know if there was anything humanly possible that could be done for her son.

The vet took one whiff of Stinky's breath and yelped, "Phewie!" He grabbed a bottle of whisky and gargled with it. "Your son has a case of what we in the trade call *halitosis gigantis* — that's big bad breath."

Then he solemnly prescribed his cure. "Ma'am, your son is a natural born cowboy. Why I've met fellows who after a week on the range had breath so bad they could knock this boy off a cliff. I don't know what they eat out there or what they do, but boy does it stink. The only thing for your Billy here is to become a cowboy."

What young fellow wouldn't be overjoyed to be told by a qualified professional to become a cowboy? Not a one, and Stinky was no exception. The very next day, after he graduated from school, he ran off into the mountains and joined up with the Rancid Bar Ranch.

The Rancid Bar Ranch was the smelliest outfit in the West. You would swear that these boys not only didn't bathe, they probably didn't even know what soap was. Their cattle brand was one thick horizontal line with five thin wavy lines coming up out of it like a bad smell. These cowboys would work far away from civilization for months at a time, and if the rodeo came into in town, all the normal citizens prayed that the Rancid Bar ranchers would stay out on the range. The only reason that anybody put up with them was because the meat that came from the Rancid Bar was the tenderest and most flavorful beef in the West. In fact, they claimed that, depending on which cowboys were tending the herd, Rancid Bar cattle came pre-smoked, and tasted like the finest beef jerky.

Now you'd think that Stinky would fit right in, but that wasn't the case. Although all the other fellows at the Rancid Bar smelled to high heaven, their smell was different. It was pungent body odor — the stink of sweat and hard work. So the other ranchers sort of looked down their noses at Stinky, and made him ride out by himself in the loneliest part of the pasture, near the edge of the forest.

Stinky didn't mind, though. He'd had enough of folks teasing and making fun of him. He did his work, and he kept the cattle safe. So they paid him cash money just like everybody else, but they made him sleep outside the bunkhouse and sit outside the chow hall, unless they were serving beans.

One time, when Stinky was in town to deposit his money into the Wells Fargo Bank, a bank robber came in for a stickup. He was more than confused when he saw that everybody else in the place already had their bandannas up over their noses, including the tellers. He pulled out his pistol anyway and barked, "This is a stickup. What's going on around here?"

Well, all Stinky did was cough in his direction. The bandit's gun fell right off its gunstock. The wood had rotted through in an instant. The gun's barrel fell to the ground, and the robber himself crashed backwards to the floor in a dead faint.

A cheer went up inside the bank, and the bank manager said he'd shake Stinky's hand as long as Stinky promised not to exhale. When the newspaper reporter interviewed him about the wondrous feat, Stinky just blushed and said he'd had a peanut butter and onion sandwich for breakfast.

He often ate strange meals, Stinky did, especially when he was out on his own. See, he figured that some day he'd find a food so powerful that the stench of the meal might knock his own stank right out of his body. He ate liverwurst and spinach, old Limburger cheese, anchovies, pickled pigs feet, any kind of old fish, beets in vinegar sauce, strange-flavored chicken, thousand-year-old eggs, and even bowls of kimchee, a foul-smelling cabbage salad from Korea that the cook made and stored in a slop bucket. It didn't work, but now the boys at the Rancid Bar made Stinky ride even further out, right on the edge of the forest, fixing fence posts and looking for lost cattle in the mountains and river valleys or up near the old Tender Lake Reservoir.

Once a month, the chow cook would load Stinky's saddle bags up with all his moldy old leftovers and whatever other strange and noxious concoctions he could devise. The odorous young man would mount his horse, which by the way had no sense of smell whatsoever, and ride off across the prairie to do his solitary duty.

It happened that one particular winter there had been a heavy snowfall. Drifts twenty feet thick weren't uncommon down in town, and up in the mountains everybody said that the peaks were now higher than Everest, just because of the extra snow.

When spring and then summer came, all that snow started melting, and the rivers grew higher and the lakes got fuller than they'd ever been before. The townsfolk even had to build the Tender Lake Dam up another seventeen feet to keep all the water inside from overflowing.

Winter had been rough, but the summer was dry. The days were long and hot. The tall grass in the fields was crackly and yellow.

One sweltering afternoon, Stinky was out, searching for a particularly stubborn calf that liked to take strolls through very diverse countryside, when he smelled something. He knew that whatever it was it had to be strong to get past the reek of his own breath (which by the way he kind of liked). He sniffed hard, and then he snuffled long. It smelled like smoke. He spotted the calf halfway up a hill, roped it and turned his horse around all in a single smooth movement.

Then he headed back down the mountain to the Rancid Bar to see what was up.

To his surprise the fields were on fire. The whole hay pasture was ablaze, and the flames was spreading towards town. It had been a dry summer, and the hay, which had been reserved to provide feed for the cattle, was burning like a meadow of match sticks.

All the ranch hands were out battling the fire with blankets and buckets of water. They were beating on the embers with their coats, but they weren't making any dent in the conflagration. The flames were so high and so hot that Stinky could feel them even though he was miles away.

At first, Stinky kicked his horse and headed in towards the ranch to see if he could be of help, but then he got an idea. He thought about it once, and then he considered it again. He decided it was a good idea, so he tied the calf to a nearby tree, spun his horse in the other direction, and raced back into the forest.

Some of the other cowboys at the Rancid Bar saw Stinky running away, and as they fought the awesome blaze, they started shouting over the roar that he was a coward. Stinky heard them, but he had lots of practice ignoring taunts. Little did they know what he had in mind.

Stinky rode hard to the base of the Tender Lake Dam. He climbed off his horse, and then he opened up his saddle bag and started to eat his lunch. He had an onion and garlic sandwich with a thick slice of twenty-five-year-old Limburger cheese, a piece of rancid gefilte fish with anchovies, and the biggest gob of kimchee that the West had ever seen. He washed it all down with a glass of skanky patent medicine he'd bought from a traveling show. The brackish beverage tasted like sewer water mixed with kerosene and sea kelp (which it very well might have been). Nevertheless, Stinky choked down every last drop.

Then he stared up at the Tender Lake Dam, and made a few calculations in his head. In those days, they didn't make dams out of boulders, concrete and cement. It was constructed from logs piled way up high. If he made a mistake, then all the cowpokes back at the Rancid Bar would be certain he was yellow.

He crinkled his nose, and started for a part of the dam that was off to the side, not quite over the creek that most of the water ran off into.

And then Stinky breathed. He breathed on those logs. He blew and he puffed. You could see the air coming out of him, because it was yellow and green.

As soon as his breath touched the logs of the dam, they turned black started to rot. The wood was falling apart. Splinters went flying. Stinky blew and blew on the dam some more, and then he paused.

He was sure that if the dam broke now, it would probably save the ranch and save the town, but he also knew for certain that he would likely drown.

He made up his mind and then he blew again. He blew again, and blew again. More logs turned moldy and black, and skinny fountains of water began to shoot out through the cracks. Then, he heard a creak and a crackle, he knew that the dam was about to burst.

Stinky jumped on his horse, turned, and he rode hard. But he breathed all along the way down the mountain, aiming his foul exhalations at trees that he passed.

The timber fell quick and fast, like Stinky was Paul Bunyan logging the great Northwest, but the wood all dropped in a row. If you'd been watching from above, you'd have been able to see what Stinky was doing, but from the ground, it looked like our hero had gone insane.

And maybe he was. You see, he was making a channel for the water to follow him down the mountain. He was huffing and puffing and driving his horse like there was no tomorrow.

Behind him, he heard the final crashing boom echo through the valley as the dam broke, and Stinky knew that water was even now spilling down the trail.

At the edge of the pasture, he stopped, jumped off his horse, and untied the terrified calf that he'd left behind, blew out of one nostril into the cow's mouth so the poor thing fell asleep, and then threw it onto the back of his horse and started riding again.

All the cowpokes at the Rancid Bar saw Stinky racing back, and they began jeering at him, but Stinky paid them no mind. He rode hard and fast, because right at his horse's tail was a wall of water that looked like a tidal wave! The water was pouring down the mountainside, straight towards the inferno, which was now taller than the Church's steeple.

Stinky aimed his horse straight into the center of the firestorm just as the flood caught up with him. In an instant both the horse and rider were lost in the massive cloud of black smoke that hissed as soon as the river water reached the edge of the burning field.

Rancid Bar Ranch hands gasped and gaped, and then they ran for cover, because the water was coming right toward them. They made for the bunkhouse, and climbed on top, but it didn't help.

The water swept through the bunkhouse and poured over them. The only way they kept from drowning was by holding onto each other and holding onto the foreman, who had his arms tight around the cook, who was hanging onto the chow hall chimney for dear life.

Well, it had been a dry summer. The ground absorbed the moisture and the flood waters receeded quickly. The creek settling back into its regular channel. The soggy hands from the Rancid Bar climbed down from the roof and looked out at the soaked hay fields.

Where was Stinky? He'd been washed away in the deluge. Was he broken, battered, smashed or drowned?

Then the cook pointed, and everyone turned and started laughing out loud.

There he was, high up on Indian Bluff Hill, still on his horse, still holding onto the unconscious calf.

They all let out a cheer, and so did the townsfolk, who had seen the fire and the rescue, and were happy because their homes and farms were saved.

That very evening, there was a barn dance, and the mayor gave Stinky two medals — one for his heroic bravery in putting out the fire and saving the town and the ranch, and the other for finally giving the Rancid Bar Ranchers the bath of their lives, cleaning them up so good that everybody could enjoy the barn dance together.

"From this day on," the Mayor proclaimed, "anybody who calls you Stinky is going to spend the night cleaning out the town's septic system. I thank you, and the town thanks you. Three cheers for Bad Breath Bill!"

Well, they all hipped and hoorayed!

Our hero didn't say nothing. He just smiled and nodded his head, because he knew if he opened his mouth, his affliction would spoil the fun.

Then, before anyone could protest, the mayor's beautiful daughter jumped up on the stage and gave him a kiss right on the lips, which surprised him so much he started sputtering.

Everyone in town held their breaths, because they were sure she was going to die.

But she didn't. She just smiled, took Bill's hand, and led him out for the first square dance.

I don't know if that kiss cured Bill for good, because the nickname stuck. With the reward money, Bad

Breath Bill bought the Rancid Bar Ranch and planted a crop of rice, which he grew at a profit that year before turning the fields back to hay as befitted a mountain pasture. He and the mayor's daughter got married, and had kids, all of whom were very distinctive in their own ways.

But that, as they say, is another story.

The Haunted Playground

WHEN I was growing up, the playground next to our house was haunted. You could tell just by looking. The trees were tall and dark and creepy. It had a high fence around it, and a gate that squeaked so loud it sounded like a scream when you opened it. The playground was built in the days when nobody cared about kids' safety. The slide was too high and too steep. The merry-go-round spun at about a hundred miles an hour. The swings were long and skinny boards suspended from two frayed ropes, and the whole swing set wobbled when you kicked your feet. The ground was cement, cracked and broken, and littered with rusty nails and scatterings of shattered glass. And the teeter-totter did exactly that. It was a fifteen foot seesaw plank of splintering wood with steel handles at both ends and a rickety hinge in the middle.

We knew it was haunted not just because it looked like a Stephen King movie nightmare set, but because of the stories about kids who had died on the playground. We had heard these stories over and over again. They were passed down from kid to kid.

My sister Ellen especially liked to torture me by telling them late at night.

She told me about Sally Sliker, a little girl who loved to slide. She was five years old when she lay on her back and sped headfirst down the slide. She slid down the cold steel slide and flew off the bottom without slowing… Her skull hit the concrete and cracked open like a sweet baby watermelon.

I gaped at Ellen. "No way."

"Yes way."

Wendy Wings liked to swing. She swung so high, she tried to reach the sky. She kicked and rocked and went higher and higher. Then one of the ropes snapped. It whipped around her neck, and she swung like a sack, back and forth until her kicking and twitching stilled.

Then there was Peter Puker. That was his nickname. He liked to spin on the merry-go-round. Round and round and round he went until his face was a blur and the whole world swirled. When he got off, he'd vomit on the ground. Then he'd hop back on for another nauseating spin. One day the merry-go-round got out of control, and he threw up his guts – literally. His intestines went flying out of his mouth, and nobody knew how to put them back in.

I asked Ellen if that was true and she said, "Swear to God."

The scariest of all was the story about Jackie Jack, the boy with two names. He had a twin brother named Johnnie. The two of them would spend hours on the seesaw, bouncing up and down, up and down, like a manic oil derrick. One day, Johnnie Jack jumped off while Jack was on his way up. The teeter board slammed down, and Jackie Jack broke his back. I believed this one because I'd been on that teeter-totter board and had my teeth jarred when Ellen jumped off.

We didn't play in that playground much. Only on the warmest and sunniest of days, and never after dark.

And never ever ever on Halloween.

Everyone in the neighborhood knew that the ghosts in the playground walked and skipped and played on Halloween.

One year, my father once suggested that we decorate the playground and make it look spooky for Halloween. We laughed nervously, and didn't even think about making that happen.

That was the year that I learned for sure that the playground was haunted.

It was Halloween. We were out trick or treating, Ellen and I. She was a roller-girl, and I was a vampire. It was a warm night and we had a good haul. My pillowcase was so heavy I had to drag it.

"I'm going home," Ellen said. "I've got enough."

Not me. There was never enough. "Dad said we could stay out until eight, and I'm not coming in until one minute before."

"Okay," Ellen said. "I'll see you later."

And off she went, home.

I smiled and flew up the walk to ring the bell of another house. And another. And another.

I was making my way back home, not really paying attention, wondering whether I could squeeze in two more houses, when I realized that I was right in front of the haunted playground's gate.

The gate creaked open. I jumped and started to back away.

Then a big black body leaped in front of me.

I almost screamed. I turned to run.

"Hey, kid, where're you going?"

I recognized the voice. It was Butch Mattingly, the biggest bully in our school. He was dressed like a Gorilla, which wasn't much of a stretch.

"Home," I said.

Butch was standing right in my way.

"You wanna play in the playground?" he said. "We can jump out and scare other kids."

"No way!" I said. "You'd have to be stupid to go into that haunted playground on Halloween."

Butch looked at me funny. "You calling me stupid?"

"I didn't mean it that way."

"Because I'm not stupid."

Then he did the meanest thing. He grabbed my pillowcase of treats, spun it around his head, and launched it up and over the fence into the playground.

"Hey!" I yelled.

"Go get it," he teased. "Nyah nyah-nyah nyah nyah."

I looked at the playground. The moon was full, but you couldn't see it through the long fingerlike branches of the trees. Then I shook my head.

"Chicken! Chicken!" Butch clucked.

I wanted to cry. I stepped out into the street to get around Butch and started to head home.

"Come on, kid. That must be twenty pounds of candy."

"You're so brave," I shouted, "you get it!"

"All right. I will. And when I do get it, I'm gonna keep it."

I stopped right there in the middle of the street, and I watched. I saw it all happen.

I saw Butch pull open the gate, which yowled like a tortured cat.

I saw him step inside.

I saw the gate close by itself with a loud creak.

"Hey, kid, cut it out," came Butch's voice from inside.

"I didn't do anything," I answered.

Then I heard the voices. They were high pitched and faint. "Play with me.... Play with me."

"Hey, where'd you kids come from?" Butch said.

Little Sally Sliker, Peter Puker. "Play with me."

"Hey, get away," came Butch's voice. "You kids should be home."

Wendy Wings said, "Over here. Play with me."

"No, no," said Jackie Jack. "Play with me."

"Hey, leggo," shouted Butch. "Leggo. Get off me!"

And then he screamed, "Yaaaaaaaaaaaaaaaaaah!"

I ran so fast I don't even remember going home.

My Dad said, "What's going on?"

"Nothing." My face was white.

"Where's your candy?"

"It's in the playground."

Dad shrugged. "Let's go get it."

"No way! You'd have to be stupid to go into that haunted playground on Halloween."

Dad gave me a hard stare. "Are you calling me stupid?"

"I didn't mean that!" I shouted, running upstairs.

"In the morning, then," Dad said, after me. "Get ready for bed."

I told Ellen the whole story, and she just smiled.

"Told you so," she said. Then she took pity on me and shared some of her loot. One single tiny Dum-Dum, butterscotch flavor.

The next morning was a Saturday, and Dad took me down to the playground.

The iron gate creaked as he opened it.

Dad went in first.

"Weird," he said. "Crazy kids."

I stopped in my tracks. I didn't go in, but I looked through the gate.

Butch's gorilla suit was scattered all over the place. One gorilla foot was at the top of the slide. Another foot was stuck on a swing. The top of the suit was on one side of the see saw, and the bottom on the other. And spinning round and around in the middle of the merry-go-round was the empty gorilla mask.

Butch Mattingly was never seen again.

The next year they bulldozed the old playground and put in a new plastic one with wood chips and rubber mats. Everything was shiny and primary colored and very very safe. Lots of kids played there, but I never did.

Because sometimes at night when my window was open I could hear the swings creaking by themselves, and to me it sounded a lot like Butch.

"Nyah nyah-nyah nyah nyah."

Abu Hassan's Mighty Wind

My Uncle Peter used to tell this story after every Thanksgiving meal, while my mother was in the kitchen doing the dishes. It was really popular with his nephews. Even Ellen couldn't help herself and giggled. He claimed he heard it when he was stationed in Iraq and that it was from the Arabian Nights.

In the city of Baghdad lived a merchant by the name of Abu Hassan. He was a big big fat man. He liked to eat and drink, and drink and eat. He would awake to breakfast, devour his way through lunch, pause for a late afternoon snack, and commence again when it was time for dinner. As for desserts, once he got started it was almost impossible for him to stop.

After many years of living alone, he decided to get married. He found a beautiful young girl, made all the arrangements with her family, and the date of the wedding was set.

On the day of the wedding, when she was at last introduced to her husband, she was shocked to see how immense he was. She was just a slip of a girl, lovely and shy. Her mother had warned her, but she hadn't imagined that she was to be the wife of a whale! Still, she smiled and said nothing, knowing that all would be as it would be.

After the wedding ceremony came the traditional feast, and at the feast Abu Hassan ate and drank, and drank and ate… Everything was so good!

And when he was done, he wiped his gigantic maw with a napkin the size of a towel.

It was traditional for the husband to give the bride a gift, and he had a wonderful present for his new wife.

"Quiet everyone! Please! I have something to give to my sweet one."

The banquet hall grew hushed. All of his friends and relatives, and all of her relatives and friends fell silent.

He stood, tottered over to the large gift box. He smiled at his wife. She blushed.

He bent down and…

BRAAAAAAAAAAAP!

Using mere letters to describe the volume of the sound and force of the breeze that emitted from Abu Hassan's backside is an exercise in futility. The glasses on the tables blew backwards. The windows in the banquet hall shattered. In the streets of the marketplace, fruit sellers covered their mouths, children pinched their noses, and even the camels scowled and sneezed. Ten miles from the city, fourteen elephants in a caravan raised their trunks and trumpeted a reply.

Inside the hall, the friends and relatives were stunned. Milk curdled, butter melted, bread, almonds, and dates grew mold, and all the cheese went rancid. Grown men coughed and gasped. Women fell to the carpeted floor in dead faints, their fingers twitching spasmodically.

Abu Hassan's wife sputtered and waved her delicate hands frantically about in front of her rosy lips and handsome aquiline nose.

For his part, Abu Hassan's eyes widened in shock and embarrassment. His face turned as red as a perfectly ripe pomegranate. He looked across the ruin of his wedding feast.

And then he fled.

He ran from his house and climbed on a camel. He rode the camel out of the city of Baghdad to the sea. He boarded a ship and he sailed across the sea to India.

There he lived the life of a wanderer, eating and drinking nothing but what he needed to survive.

After ten years, he began to wonder what had become of his wife.

He boarded a ship and sailed across the sea. He hired a camel and rode back to the city of Baghdad. He left the camel at the gate and walked through its ancient streets.

"I wonder," he thought, "if anyone remembers me after so many years."

At last he came to the street where he had lived. His magnificent palace was at the far end. He was nearly home.

Just then, he passed a little girl sitting on the steps of her home. Her mother was sitting behind her, picking lice out of the little girl's hair.

"Mother, a friend of mine wants to tell my fortune," the little girl said. "I wonder if you can tell me when I was born."

"Little one, don't you remember, I told you," the mother answered with a laugh. "You were born in the very year, on the very day, at the very moment of Abu Hassan's mighty fart."

Abu Hassan stopped in the middle of the street. His blood went cold because he realized that not only had no one forgotten what had happened, they had probably made it into a national holiday!

He very nearly turned and fled back to India, but his house was so close…

He forced his legs to move down the street. He climbed the steps and knocked at the door.

A beautiful woman opened the door.

Abu Hassan looked up and smiled. "My wife!"

"Who are you?" A voice like honey came from her beautiful red lips.

"It is I, your husband, Abu Hassan," he answered.

She stared and frowned, her lips curving like a scimitar. "You are not my husband. My husband was a big big fat man. You are nothing but a skinny old beggar. Go away."

She began to shut the door, but Abu Hassan shouted. "No, it is I, Abu Hassan! I have been away in India. I have eaten nothing, I have drunk nothing but what I needed to survive for the past ten years. How can I prove to you I am who I say?"

She stared. "I can only think of one way that my husband could prove to me he was who he said."

Abu Hassan sighed. He turned. He bent over and…

BRRRAAAAAAAAAPP!

They say that the door to Abu Hassan's house was warped beyond repair. They say that all of the lice in the little girl's hair died and fell to the ground.

They say that Abu Hassan's wife gasped. They say that her brown eyes turned purple and her olive complexion turned pale yellow. They say that at last she choked out the words, "My husband!" Then she collapsed into his waiting arms.

And they lived, as all people do, until the end of their days.

Ellen vs. the Snakes

Chapter One
Snake Phobia

This is a story of the fights between brothers and sisters, of cruelty, revenge, fear, danger and heroism. It's about adventure, wilderness, destruction and redemption. It's why, even though I have problems with my sister Ellen, I can't help but love her too. But before we get to that, let me start at the beginning…

My sister Ellen hates snakes. I love them. This is a basic and wonderful conflict.

Ellen is two years older than me, and like most older sisters do, she drives me crazy. Once she superglued all the drawers in my desk closed, and when I finally pried them open with a crowbar, I found that she'd managed to put them in upside down, so that all my papers and things came crashing out onto the floor. My Dad didn't believe that was her fault. He said it seemed more like something that I would have done to her. Another time, she drove me to the mall and left me there. Later she claimed that she just forgot, but try telling that to me — the kid who ran down four flights of parking lot stairs screaming for her to stop and then watching and panting as our car patched out as it headed home. She didn't get in trouble for that either. My parents love my sister. They tolerate me.

The truth is that I can be pretty wicked to her, and I do like playing pranks and tricks. Can you blame me? She's bigger, older, has more friends, more money and my parents love her more. I call it "justifiable cruelicide." My biggest problem isn't thinking up new and horrible tortures. Any boy on the planet can devise evil and non-lethal ways to deal with a brother or sister. The real challenge is getting away with it — making my own behavior in the circumstances seem totally legal and justifiable, or even better, invisible.

Her fear of snakes, for example, is totally my fault. I used to take great pride in that.

It started when we got a pet snake in our science classroom. Our teacher, Professor Sinkovitz, rescued it from his swimming pool. It was only a common garter snake, but we still thought it was the coolest thing. The day the Prof brought it in he explained to us in his weird German-Texan accent, "It would haff to been killed by the chlorine, pardners." It was eighteen inches long with a checkered back and a darting tongue. The Prof kept it in a nearly empty fish tank with a branch and a heat lamp.

Every morning all the guys would run over and see what it had eaten. We filled its tank with crickets, grasshoppers, aphids, ladybugs, slugs and even tiny baby mice. Sometimes you could see the critters it was digesting still kicking around. Talk about science!

At dinner time, when our family gathered to feed, my father insisted that "Everybody needs to tell something about their day." He really wanted to hear something new that we learned, but over the years, he had given up and settled for bits of news like, "I lost my sneaker in the mud near the gym and had to wear one shoe and one sock all day, so we need to buy me some new ones by tomorrow or else I can't compete in the track meet." (That one, believe it or not, was Ellen's, and I didn't believe it. Ellen didn't think her sneakers weren't fast enough, so she'd lost one on purpose. Then, because she competed in new sneakers, she lost the race and came home with a blister the size of my thumb.)

The day the snake arrived, I couldn't wait to talk about it at dinner.

"He's got a checkered back," I said, "so we call him King Henry the Eighth."

My mother looked puzzled. "That doesn't make any sense. Why don't you kids call him Checkers?"

I rolled my eyes. "Because Henry the Eighth played chess and ate everything in sight!"

My dad nodded. "That makes sense."

Ellen, however, kept mum, which was weird because she usually liked to rag on anything and everything I said.

"He doesn't wriggle either," I explained. "He slithers."

"Now I don't understand," Dad said. "I thought snakes wriggled."

"Nope," I shook my head. "Eels wriggle and writhe. They twist and turn. Snakes oscillate and slither. We looked it up in the dictionary."

Dad pursed his lips. "I'm pretty sure that snakes can wriggle and writhe in addition to slithering."

"Well, it sounds like you're learning a lot in school these days," Mom said, heading off any argument.

Ellen was still quiet. She was staring at her food, not touching a bite.

I grinned. "Great spaghetti, Mom!"

That's when I realized that Ellen was afraid. She kept quiet because she knew that if I knew I would do everything in my power to torture her.

Later on, I did some research in the dictionary. The general name for a fear of lizards was herpetophobia. The specific clinical name for the fear of snakes was ophidiophobia. But if you looked up a picture of my sister Ellen on the Internet, you'd find it right beside the words, snake phobia.

Which was why I volunteered to take King Henry the Eighth home over Thanksgiving vacation.

Chapter Two
Snake in a Box

Dad picks me up from school every Wednesday. It's great. We get to hang out together and not say much. He usually asks me how things are going, and I say, "Fine." Then I ask how he's doing and he says, "The usual," and then we go bowling. Or to the movies. Or play video games at this high priced arcade and restaurant. It's cool.

We started the whole thing when I complained that the guys who had divorced parents spent more time with their dads than I did.

Mom always says, "Did you boys have a good time?"

We both say, "Yeah."

Then she whispers to Dad, "Did you two talk at all this time?" Like I don't have good hearing because I'm the only one in the family too young to have blown out my eardrums at rock concerts.

Dad shrugs and we eat dinner.

Anyway, the day before Thanksgiving, when Dad picked me up, I told him that I needed help. We had to go back to my classroom to get something. He shuffled along behind me, pretending to admire the lame-o art on the school walls.

When we finally got to the science classroom, Prof Sink was standing outside, tapping his foot and looking at his watch.

"Howdy volks. It is good for you to do this thing for this here ranch," the Prof said to Dad.

Professor Sinkovitz had been born in Germany, but moved to our school from somewhere in Texas.

"Sure," Dad said, shrugging. He never understands a word the Prof says. It took all us kids about three months before we realized that he was actually speaking English to us.

"The critter varmint is here inside," the Prof said, leading us to the back of the room. "This box should to keep him until he is to be transferred to the heated receptacle. He haff already been too well fed on small furry mouse-icle today, so in almost probability will not need more mealing until after brought back to school."

The Prof patted a closed cardboard box. Plastered on the outside in dark black letters were the words, "CAUTION: LIVE ANIMAL"

"Huh?" Dad said.

"The snake is in the box and it's been fed," I translated. "I'm going to keep him in that old aquarium we have in the basement."

Dad stared at the box. He stared at me. "Did you ask Mom?"

Prof Sink may sound like he's insane, but he's pretty sharp on the uptake. He had asked the kids in school if anyone could take care of the snake over the long weekend because he knew that as a cost-saving measure the heat in the building was being turned down to just above freezing. He was traveling to Alabama and was already running late. "Is there to be a big problem?"

"Dad, please!" I begged. (Ellen's not the only one who knows how to turn on the charm and guilt. She's just better at it than me.)

Dad sighed and slumped and nodded. "No. It's fine. Can I at least look at him first?"

"You want to look at snake in box?"

"Sure," Dad said. "Why not?"

The Professor knew that this was a deal breaker, so he nodded to Dad, and then winked at me.

As soon as Dad lifted the lid off the box, the Professor yelled, "Watch out for snake!"

Dad jumped back about three feet and dropped the box to the floor.

King Henry the Eighth slithered out onto the linoleum and looked annoyed.

Both the Prof and I burst out laughing. I gave the Prof a high five. He said, "See you to Monday. Enjoy your Dead Turkey Day." And was gone.

I picked up King Henry, put him back in the box, and put the lid on.

That's when I noticed Dad wasn't smiling. He was glaring. He was angry.

"What?" I said.

"What was that all about?" he snapped. He kept his voice down, but I knew that if we were at home he'd be yelling at me.

"It's a classroom tradition!" I quickly explained. "Whenever somebody opens a box with a snake in it, everybody else shouts, 'Watch out for snake!' You get scared the first time, but it's kind of like a traveling practical joke. After that first time, you get to startle somebody else. Don't blame me. The Prof did it to you."

At last Dad shook his head, smiled and even started to laugh a little. We lugged the box to the car, put King Henry in the back seat, and went to an indoor archery range. Shooting bows and arrows is fun, but not as easy as it looks in the movies or cartoons. I didn't get a single bull's-eye, but I did manage to hit the target pretty consistently by the end of the session.

When we got home, I ran into the house to start my homework and Dad brought the box into the kitchen.

In my school, when you have a long weekend, the teachers give you extra homework because you have extra time. I was going to get it all done Wednesday night so I wouldn't have to cram at the last minute.

I was upstairs working on a math word problem when it happened.

There was a loud piercing shriek. "AAAAAAAAAAAH!"

Then a crash.

Then a curse.

Then uncontrollable sobbing.

I ran downstairs to the kitchen. It was horrible!

There was blood everywhere. Ellen was curled in the corner. My mother stood next to the stove with a knife in her hand. My dad was on his knees. His hands were red.

I gasped. My eyes were wide. I didn't know whether to scream or run, call an ambulance or the police.

Mom saw what was going through my mind, set down the knife and in a calm voice said, "Relax. Nobody's hurt. When Ellen saw the snake in the box, she screamed and I dropped a jar of spaghetti sauce. Your Dad is picking up the broken glass. Why don't you look for your reptile? I think it went into the living room. Dinner is going to be late."

A second look at the scene and I realized that everything was okay. Now I saw the box on the floor on the far side of the kitchen table. Ellen was clearly upset. It was not the time to ask more questions.

While I was searching under the couch on my hands and knees, Dad wandered by and whispered, "You owe me one."

I had no idea what he meant at the time. I found King Henry curled up near the radiator. Dinner was incredibly late. Nobody said a word. Not even what we'd learned that day. Just before lights out, Dad sneaked into my room and swore me to secrecy.

"I was helping your mother make dinner," he explained. "Ellen was peeking under the lid of the box."

"You didn't," I gasped.

He nodded. "I did."

Dad had yelled, "Watch out for snake!"

Ellen had screamed and the tomato sauce bloodbath was the result.

We both covered our mouths and laughed silently until our sides ached.

It's so sweet when I can torture my sister and cause chaos without taking any of the blame.

Chapter Three
Snakes on a Platter

My mom told her sister about the great snake tableau, and Aunt Dorothy told Uncle Peter, who told his son. So naturally, when they came over for Thanksgiving, Adam brought his new snake.

My cousin Adam is one of my best friends. But even though we live in the same town and go to the same school, it sometimes seems like we never get to hang out together. We'd been looking forward to the long weekend for months.

When Adam showed up at the door with a boa constrictor draped over his shoulders, I pretty much shouted, "NO WAY!"

"Yessah!" Adam nodded and grinned like a beaver with glasses.

"Ellen, come here," I yelled. "You've gotta see this."

She was in the kitchen in the middle of basting the turkey. She came into the front hall in her apron, saw the snake, and squirted turkey juice all over the wall. Her face was dead white pale as she ran up the stairs.

Adam and I burst into laughter. Even Uncle Morris was chuckling.

"That was so mean," Aunt Dorothy said, struggling through the front door with a box full of pies. "Adam, I told you that you had to put that thing away and not tease Ellen with it."

"I didn't tease her," Adam said. "It's not my fault."

"Mine either. I didn't mean to," I said. "I just thought she should know about it..."

Aunt Dorothy didn't buy it for a second. "Put the snake away and start washing the walls."

Still giggling, we brought Adam's snake, which he called Crusher, down to the basement and put him in the heated aquarium with King Henry the Eighth. After making sure that the two crowded snakes wouldn't eat each other, (which we were kind of hoping they would at least try) we grabbed sponges and warm soapy water and started our chore.

It's not easy getting turkey grease off a clean white wall. By the time we were done to my mother's satisfaction, it was dinner time.

As was our tradition, we sat around the table and said what we were thankful for.

Uncle Morris started. "I'm thankful to be alive."

"I'm thankful I have legs," Adam said.

"I'm thankful I have warm blood," I said.

"I'm thankful I don't have a gun," Ellen said, "because I'd shoot you both!"

"Ellen…" Mom warned. "Say something nice."

She muttered something about being thankful for a nice dinner.

When it was my father's turn, he looked around the table with a broad smile and said, "I'm thankful that we're all here today, and that some of us will be going to Africa soon."

Adam's head shot up and his eyes darted from my Dad to his Dad. Adam's father, my Uncle Peter, was still a reserve Colonel in the army, and Adam had been moving around the world all his life.

"No." Uncle Peter shook his head. "Not us. I haven't received orders that I know of."

"Mom?" Adam asked. "What?"

"I don't know anything about this either," Aunt Dorothy said.

"Tell them already," my mother said to my father.

Dad's smile got even wider. "Kids, we're going on a family trip to Africa."

"No way!" I gasped.

"When?" Ellen said.

"Winter vacation," Dad said. "In fact, we're pulling you guys out of school two days early because we got a great rate on a flight."

Ellen's face dropped like a rock, and I knew why. She'd been dying to ask my parents if she could go on a ski vacation with her friend Ashley. Ashley's family had a chalet in Vermont, and Ashley also had an older brother that Ellen was sweet on.

"This is so awesome!" I said, punching Adam in the shoulder.

"Absolutely," Adam said, punching me back.

"Do I have to go?" Ellen said.

"Yes," my mother said. "We all have to go. This is a wonderful opportunity for us to see the world and spend some time together as a family."

"I can't believe this!" Ellen burst into tears and ran from the table.

"Well," Dad said, "that went rather poorly."

We all finished thankfulness, blessed the food, and dug in. Eventually, Mom went upstairs to Ellen's room and talked her down. Her face was red and puffy. Adam and I were careful to avoid eye contact with her.

The meal was magnificent. I love everything having to do with Thanksgiving from the turkey and stuffing to the gravy and even the canned cranberry sauce.

After dinner but before dessert we have another family tradition — nap time. Nobody cleans up. We leave all the dishes for later and everybody pretty much waddles away from the table and finds a quiet place to bunk down for an hour. Sometimes the guys doze in front of the television, pretending to watch the games. Ellen had offered Aunt Dorothy and Uncle Peter her bed. Adam and I went up to my room and lay on the floor in sleeping bags like we were camping out. We talked for a while and were just snoozing off when once again the screaming began.

I don't know if you've ever been woken from a deep nap by a series of piercing shrieks, but it sets your heart racing like an alarm bell clanging inside your chest.

Adam and I were on our feet and out my bedroom and down the stairs before we were fully conscious.

Later on, I realized that horror films have at least one element of truth in them. You know the scenes where you watch as the poor idiot is going down the hall and about to open the door that you know the horrible monster is behind? You're sitting in your seat squirming and thinking, "Don't do it!" And later on you can't believe that anybody would be so dumb to keep going knowing that there was evil just around the corner…

We were listening to this horrible noise and none of us stopped to think.

The screaming got louder and louder as we pounded down the stairs to the basement and banged through the cellar door.

It was hard to see. The only light in on the underground room came from a weak bulb on the ceiling. There was a shape. A writhing, moving thing. A person. A screaming shrieking girl.

It was Ellen. She was covered in snakes. Dozens of little snakes, some of them three inches, some of them nearly a foot long. They were squirming all over her body, wriggling on her shoulders, twisting through her hair. She was trying to pull them off and throw them on the ground, but every time she dropped one, another one appeared.

"What the heck is going on?" my father's voice came from behind us.

"The snakes have given birth!" Adam said.

"Are they dangerous?" my mother and Aunt Dorothy asked simultaneously.

"No," said Adam and I (also simultaneously).

"Help me!" Ellen gasped.

The two of us rushed forward and began plucking the baby reptiles off my sister and dropping them back into the aquarium.

As soon as she was clean, Ellen collapsed, sobbing into my mother's arms.

She explained that she was just trying to face her fears. She'd actually picked up both snakes and was looking at them, when all of a sudden snakes started shooting out everywhere. It seemed like the whole room was full of snakes.

Mom took her upstairs and promised her the first slice of pecan pie.

Aunt Dorothy looked like she wanted to berate us for teasing Ellen, but it was blatantly obvious that we had nothing to do with it. All she could do was demand that we check the room for any missing snakes, turn on her heel and march upstairs to comfort my sister.

Dad and Uncle Peter had their hands over their mouths, and as soon as all the women were gone, the guys all cracked up.

"I always thought snakes laid eggs," Uncle Peter said.

"Not all of them," I explained. "We're studying snakes in school. Some of them give birth to live babies. Obviously both garter snakes and boas do."

"Boys," Dad said, trying to control himself. "This has to stop. We can't keep traumatizing your sister like this."

"It wasn't our fault," Adam and I said together.

"I agree," Uncle Peter giggled. "Ellen did it to herself. Still, we have to give her credit for trying."

The grown-ups went upstairs.

Adam and I got down on our hands and knees and began scouring the basement for missing infant snakes. They were tiny and tricky to catch. By the time we were done, we counted twenty-three tiny garter snakes and twelve baby boas.

"Whoah, that's a lot of snakes!" Adam said. "I knew Crusher was a girl, but I didn't know she was pregnant!"

"Yeah," I agreed. "Next week in school, we're going to have to give King Henry a new name."

"Hey," Adam's eyes lit up. "You think your sister would like a snake for a birthday present?"

It took us a long time before we stopped laughing enough to head to the dining room for dessert. By then, Ellen was upstairs in her room. Probably in bed with the covers pulled up over her head.

Chapter Four
Out to Africa

When Dad dropped me off at school after Thanksgiving with a whole box full of snakes, the principal went crazy. Her name was Mrs. Dernaski, and she was three years from retirement. She called the health department and they confiscated the whole box. Prof Sink had to go down to the city pound to retrieve it. Everybody was mad at me, and when the kids voted, instead of re-naming King Henry after one of his decapitated wives, they named her Scooter. The Prof told us to "Say a good so-long to these here rustlers." Then he sold Scooter and the little snakes to a pet store. We had a pizza party with the proceeds, which was nice but not as cool as snakes.

In the meantime, my immediate family was in a tizzy about getting ready for our Africa Experience, as my Dad took to calling it. I went to the school library and checked out every book on African reptiles I could find, including one that had a whole chapter on the African rock python, which climb trees and eat monkeys!

They say that travel is supposed to be broadening, but they don't tell you that preparing for travel is a horrible nightmare. Maybe in the old days all you had to do was sneak on a ship with your rucksack and sail away. Today you need passports, visas, and shots. Lots of shots. I needed to get vaccines for yellow fever, hepatitis A and B, typhoid and rabies, which was kind of cool because even if my arm was sore, at least I knew that if I got bit by a mad dog I wouldn't go insane. At the same time, we had to start taking anti-malarial drugs, which tasted awful.

I did some reading, and found out that there were tons of diseases in Africa that you couldn't do anything about, like dengue fever, river blindness, sleeping sickness, and even the plague!

At dinner, when I told my parents about my research, Mom looked almost as unhappy as Ellen. She went out the next day and bought a gallon of military-strength bug repellent to keep away the tsetse flies.

They also say that getting there is half the fun. Ha! Whoever made that up never had to fly through Chicago at Christmas time. We got stuck for a day, missed two connections, and ended up running full-speed through Heathrow, just in time to miss another connection. Then we sat in Cairo's airport for another sixteen hours before getting the last four seats on an overnight flight through a thunderstorm on an antique prop plane to Kilimanjaro International Airport.

We arrived in Tanzania at six in the morning, completely shattered. My parents and my sister had been nauseous for hours. Crashes of thunder shook the plane. There were no shades on the windows, so you saw lightning flashing by, and the engines looked like they were going to fall off. Nobody had slept a wink on that airplane.

Dad wanted to go straight on to our safari, but because we were nearly two days late, the guide didn't show up to meet us.

Mom made Dad check us into a hotel near the airport, which only had one room available with two twin beds. Ellen and I had to share, but somehow we managed to get to sleep without arguing.

I woke up first, jumped out of bed to get away from my sister, and went into the bathroom to read some of my new favorite book — *Killer Snakes.*

So far, I thought, this trip was a bad idea.

Then I opened the blinds to our hotel balcony, and saw the far-off peak of Mount Kilimanjaro. There was a sliver of snow on its summit. A bird that I had never seen before flew by. It looked like a vulture! There were coconut trees, and I saw a monkey climbing in them.

My face broke into a wide grin.

"We're in Africa!" I shouted.

Mom and Dad groaned. Ellen threw a pillow at me. I didn't care.

I slid the window open and stepped outside. It was sweltering hot. Without air conditioning, my clothes got wet and sticky almost immediately. I didn't care. I waved at the monkey and it waved back.

It took us another couple of hours to get breakfast. I ordered eggs and toast with a sliced pineapple on the side. Americans aren't supposed to drink the water in Africa. Our digestive systems can't take the bacteria, so I had a tall glass of iced cold grapefruit soda called Ting. Mom and Dad had coffee. Ellen was a spoilsport and ordered bottled water. When we were done, we went back to the room to repack our bags, and left them at the front desk. Then we made our way down to the marketplace. That was where our guide's office was located.

Tanzania is in East Africa, on the Indian Ocean, south of Kenya and north of Mozambique. It was formed in 1964 out of two British colonies, Zanzibar and Tanganyika. It has some of the most amazing nature preserves in the world, where herds of wild animals roam free and protected from hunters.

It's also one of the poorest countries in the world. As soon as we left our hotel, we were surrounded by beggars.

I felt horrible and over-privileged. There were all these little kids, my age and even younger. They'd stick out their hands and ask for money. Sometimes they'd try to sell us gum and things like that. I emptied my pockets of change in about two minutes. Mom said she understood, but that giving them my money would only encourage them. Dad said I needed to keep my wallet in my pocket so nobody would steal it. Ellen tried to ignore them.

We found our way to the guide's office, which was nothing more than a little shack leaning against an old building. The sign above the door read, "Tip Top Safari Tours - low budget, high quality. Nyoka G. Smith, Proprietor."

"Hey, cool!" I said. "You know what Nyoka means in Swahili?"

Ellen rolled her eyes. "Now you're a linguist?"

"I know a few words." I glared. "It means 'snake.'"

Ellen sighed. "You are really beginning to get on my nerves!"

Mom said that maybe we ought to go and hire somebody more reputable, but Dad argued that he'd already wired a deposit, and at least we should try to get a refund.

"You're all being silly," Dad said, opening the door.

Chapter Five
Some Ting Is Wrong

Inside, the Tip Top Safari office looked worse than the outside. There were three uncomfortable-looking chairs in front of a spindly desk covered completely with the hulking shape of an unconscious man.

"Oh, I'm sorry," Dad said. "We seem to be in the wrong place."

Almost instantly the man's head popped up. "No trouble at all!"

The man was a large African fellow, with closely cropped hair, a brilliant white smile, and jagged scars on each cheek. His voice was incongruously soft and pleasant, with a distinctive British accent.

"Are you the Doctor and the Family? I am Nyoka Smith. I have been waiting for you. I asked your hotel to call me when you checked out, but clearly you have found me. Well done."

He stood up and we all stepped back. He was at least six foot five. He wore a sweat-covered David Bowie tee shirt, long khaki slacks, and black Doc Marten boots.

Noticing that we all seemed startled, he held his arms wide, hands open, as if showing us that he had no weapons and we had nothing to fear.

"I see that you are deceived by my appearance. Do not be. I am Zanzibarian by birth, English by education, Oxfordian by degree, and Tanzanian by inclination. I am also the best safari guide that you will find at the price you can afford."

"Yes," my father said, still uncertain about how to proceed. "However, my family and I are exploring other arrangements."

Nyoka dropped down into his chair, which creaked precariously. "All right. Fine. I understand that Americans are often prejudiced against black people."

"That's not it at all!" my father quickly said.

"No, certainly not," my mother said.

"You're scary looking," I admitted.

His face snapped toward me. His eyes focused on me. And then his mouth widened into a smile. "Honesty is a good thing, young fellow. You do need, however, to be careful what you say from time to time."

"Look, I'm sorry," my father began.

Nyoka waved his hand as if brushing away a fly. "Nonsense. I do understand. I will simply sell your tent camp reservations in the middle of the preserve to the next interested buyer. It is, as you know, high season and these sites are few, but I expect I shall still turn a profit and I will not have to ferry and pamper a gaggle of frightened tourists."

"Stop it!" Ellen said, suddenly.

We all turned to look at her. It was unusual for Ellen to say anything in front of strangers.

"You are all being very childish," she said. "We are already days late. We have less than a week left before we have to fly back home. We don't have time to waste looking for another guide. Mr. Smith, do you promise not to rob or murder us?"

Nyoka smiled again. "But of course. In fact, I will protect you from anyone, with my life."

"Dad, do you promise to relax and trust this man?"

Dad hemmed and hawed. "I don't know."

Ellen put her hands on her hips. "If you didn't want to have an adventure and meet new people then why did you drag us to Africa?"

Mom looked at Dad. "She has a point, you know."

Dad frowned, and then looked sheepish. "You're right," he told Ellen. Then he looked at the safari guide behind his desk. "You're right, too. I was allowing myself to be prejudiced by your appearance. I am sorry."

Dad stuck out his right hand. Nyoka let it hang there for a moment, then grabbed it and began pumping.

"Not at all," he said. "It is a rare quality to admit that you are wrong, to admit that you have been foolish, to admit that you have been a racist. I have spent years in the white world, and I do understand. It is difficult to overcome. But if I can do it there, you can do it here. All is forgiven. Shall we go now?"

Dad wasn't quite sure what to make of this, but he agreed. Behind the office, Nyoka had a brand new Range Rover with this amazing roof that rose up so you could look outside at the animals without getting out of the car. We went back to the hotel, collected our bags, and then we were officially on safari!

While we bounced down a road out of town, I nudged Ellen in the ribs and whispered, "Ellen likes Nyoka."

"Shut up or I'll drop a scorpion down your underpants," she hissed back.

From the front, Nyoka called, "Scorpions are rarely fatal, young miss. I would recommend a black mambo snake. They are quite deadly, and their venom is terribly fast acting."

Ellen shuddered.

I grinned.

Then, all of a sudden, I felt sick.

"Pull over," I said.

Dad's head shot around. "Do you see a lion? An elephant?"

"It would not be unusual," Nyoka said, "to see a wildebeest so close to the town, but the lions tend to stay away.

"Pull over!" I said. "Fast!"

He pulled the car over to the side. I opened my door, and hurled my breakfast all over the dry African soil.

"What's the matter?" Ellen nudged me. "Can't take a bumpy ride?"

When I was done, Nyoka handed me a towel and a bottle of water. "You must drink so you do not become dehydrated."

"I'm okay," I said.

"What did you have for breakfast?" he asked. I told him. "I like Ting myself. Did you drink it from the bottle?"

"No," I said. "A glass with ice."

"Oh no!" my father said, smacking his forehead with his palm.

Nyoka nodded. "I'm afraid so. Young sir, when you are advised not to drink the water, next time, also do not drink the ice."

Chapter Six
Ellen vs. the Snake

I wish I could say that I had a wonderful time in Africa. I wish I could say that it was a life-changing experience, that it connected me deeply with an appreciation for the biodiversity of the planet and the wonders of life. I wish I could say that I made new friends and had so many experiences that I can't wait to go back.

Instead I was sick as a dog — a very sick dog — a skinny old flea-ridden flatulent mangy cur with sores and… Well, you get the idea.

The drive to our campsite was a blur. We stopped seven more times and I vomited eight. (Ellen was furious at me for ruining her new safari blouse, but Mom said that it was drip-dry and the bile would wash out. Mom was right, but Ellen still refused to wear the shirt again.)

I tried to keep hydrated, but everything that went down came back up. There wasn't enough bottled water in the car, which Dad joked was a good thing because if Nyoka had ten gallons of water, we'd have never made it to our campsite.

Dad's a doctor, but his bedside manner with me has always been a bit on the insensitive side. Most of his patients are terminally ill. I simply wasn't that sick, and he didn't know how to relate. He said that I didn't have any of the symptoms of malaria or sleeping sickness or the plague, and that the symptoms had arrived too quickly for those anyway. Probably I just had travelers' diarrhea, and would be better in a day or so.

Mom was more sympathetic. She held my hand and changed the barf bucket, and gave me fresh bottles of water.

Ellen, of course, was furious. Not only was I ruining her clothing, I was ruining the whole trip. And she had to share the tent with me.

The next day, when I was still too sick to travel, Nyoka convinced my family that I would be all right with the camp attendants, and they left me there.

I was all alone in the middle of Africa, running a fever, vomiting, and trying to stay hydrated. One of the kids whose parents worked at the camp brought me a radio, but the only station it picked up was playing disco and it was in the middle of a Bay City Rollers marathon.

I wanted to die.

I was having nightmares about snakes crawling out of my breakfast and guys on roller skates chasing me through school. In one dream they caught me, held me down, pulled out cans of hair spray and…

One morning I woke up, looked out the window of my tent and saw a giraffe walk by.

For a moment I was sure that I was dreaming or delusional, but then I looked around and realized that I really wasn't home. I was in Africa!

The tent I was being sick in wasn't the kind of pup tent I was used to on camping trips. It was more like a small hotel room with a wooden floor and a canvas roof and walls. We had two beds, two dressers, two tables and two easy chairs. There was electricity, a small refrigerator, and a sink with running water that I was careful not to touch. There was a front door and a door to a flush toilet and shower room. My parents' tent was next door. They had a king sized bed, so Ellen really couldn't have slept there.

Every evening my family returned from their expedition, breathless and amazed. They told me in endless details about all the wild animals they had seen.

"There was a herd of hippos by the river," Mom said. "All around them were other animals, like gazelles and flamingos. We saw a crocodile, but they don't usually bother the hippos, although they might try to eat the babies."

"I saw a whole family of baboons walking down the middle of the road. They were holding hands," Dad said. "It was like watching a weird tribe of people."

"We saw a lion with blood on his paws!" Ellen said. "It was fresh from a kill."

"No way," I whispered.

"Yes way," Ellen said, nodding her head.

It wasn't fair. I wanted to go on safari, but every morning Dad would take my temperature and shake his head. I could tell that Mom was getting worried, but Dad explained to her that I was gradually getting better. She wanted to stay with me, but he argued that this was her chance to fill her list of birds. Before she had us kids, Mom used to be an avid bird watcher. That evening she came back and told me she'd seen a secretary bird. Her eyes twinkled. Everyone was so happy.

I wasn't. I read my entire winter reading list in three days, and then had to read this horrible historical romance that Ellen brought with her about some Scottish guy in a kilt, who kept winning women and then leaving them, because his childhood sweetheart and true love was married to somebody else. The sword fights were cool, but the sex scenes probably kept me sick. Eventually they got together, but I really hoped that they lived miserably ever after.

My fever finally broke on the evening of the last full day we were in the preserve. Mom convinced Nyoka to take me out for a quick ride, but we didn't get too far.

My stomach still ached. I saw a giant termite mound, some monkeys in trees, and waaay off in the distance were a bunch of lions lying on rocks. Maybe if we'd been able to get closer I would have felt less like I was just inside a big zoo.

I managed to eat a little spaghetti with butter for dinner, and kept it down.

That night I finally slept well, and I woke up at dawn.

I'd been so sick that I hadn't really heard all the birds and animals squawking and calling. It wasn't very light yet, so I kept my eyes closed and tried to listen. This was my last chance to have a real African experience. It was more than the call of nature — it was a cacophony. I heard all different kinds of birds. I heard a roar, and then another, and then a bellow, which sounded like a hippo. I think I heard the trumpet of an elephant and the screech of a monkey, maybe a whole family of monkeys.

And then I heard a hiss.

It was loud. It was right by my left ear. My eyes shot open.

The snake was staring into my left eyeball. Its eyes were black. Its skin was dark grey with a lighter grey snout. Its tongue was tickling at my cheek.

"Ellen," I whispered, talking out of the right side of my mouth. "Ellen, there's a snake on my pillow."

"Shut up," she said.

"Ellen," I repeated, as softly as I could. "There's a snake on my pillow."

She sat up, picked up her pillow and was about to hurl it at me.

"No, please!" I whispered.

She squinted in the early morning light. Then she saw the snake, and Ellen froze for what seemed like an eternity.

The snake finished butterfly kissing my cheek, and began slithering past my nose toward my gaping open mouth, which probably looked like a hole big enough to crawl into. I didn't dare close my mouth. I didn't dare move.

Ellen sighed, stood, and grabbed the snake right behind its jaws. Her hand just snatched out and she was holding it! The tail of the snake began writhing in Ellen's bare hands. It was about three feet long and as thick as my arm.

Its mouth opened wide, and I looked inside, seeing only blackness, fangs and death.

Ellen shook her head at the snake, opened the door, and threw it as far as she could.

"There," she said.

"Is it gone?" I hissed.

"It's gone," she answered. "It bounced, and then undulated away. Are you satisfied?"

"Ellen." I sat up. "That was a black mambo."

"So?" She rolled her eyes and put her hands on her hips. "Next you're going to say it's the most poisonous snake on earth."

"Yes," I nodded my head. "One of the most poisonous, and black mambos are one probably the fastest snakes on earth. They get see you, they kill you, and you die. There's not even time for an antidote."

"So, I guess I saved your life?"

I nodded. "Thanks."

"Really?" She put her hands on her hips, looked out the door and squinted. "Hey, maybe I'm not afraid of snakes after all. Cool." Then she smiled and she looked happier and stronger than she had in a long time. "Hey, little brother, come here. Look at this."

I lifted myself out of bed and slowly made my way to the door.

Off in the distance, walking through the grassland as the sun rose,dict were seven elephants and twelve giraffes. There was a herd of gazelles and a pack of wildebeests.

We didn't really talk any more about what happened. I thanked her again, and she shrugged. We both agreed not to tell Mom and Dad about the snake.

Then Ellen and I got quiet, and sat together on the steps outside our tent, and watched the long parade of animals moving across the African horizon until the sun was high in the sky, and it was time to pack up and go back home.

About the Author

Mark Binder is the author of the novel, ***The Brothers Schlemiel,*** and a collection of stories for young people called ***The Bed Time Story Book.*** His book, ***A Hanukkah Present,*** was the finalist for the National Jewish Book Award for Family Literature.

He has edited newspapers and magazines. Mark is also an award-winning recording artist.

A graduate of Columbia University and the Trinity Rep Conservatory, he has degrees in theater, English and mythology. He once ran for the U.S. House of Representatives and got more votes per dollar spent campaigning than any candidate since 1864. He sometimes teaches and practices Aikido, the martial art for peace.

He tours the United States sharing his stories and love of the written and spoken word with people of all ages. He has performed on stage and in theaters, classrooms, festivals, community centers, churches, synagogues and even in parking lots.

He is the founder of the American Story Theater, and occasionally teaches a college course called "Telling Lies."

Mark lives with his three children in Providence, Rhode Island.

For the most recent
books, audio, weblog and stories by
Mark Binder
plus information about his
touring schedule and
entertaining and educational programs
please visit
www.markbinder.com

We hope you enjoyed
It Ate My Sister

Please look for Mark Binder's other works

BOOKS

The Brothers Schlemiel
The Bed Time Story Book
A Hanukkah Present
The Council of Wise Women

AUDIO

Adventures with Giants and Slugs
Classic Stories for Boys and Girls
Tall Tales, Whoppers and Lies
Dead at Knotty Oak
A Chanukkah Present
The Brothers Schlemiel From Birth to Bar Mitzvah

These fine books and audio recordings are available by ordering directly from your local bookstore or favorite online provider, including Amazon.Com, CDBaby.com, and the iTunes music store.

You may also order autographed copies from
www.lightpublications.com

Have an excellent day!

Breinigsville, PA USA
03 April 2011
259001BV00001B/9/P